MIRIAM

MIRIAM

Beatrice Gormley

EERDMANS BOOKS FOR YOUNG READERS
GRAND RAPIDS, MICHIGAN / CAMBRIDGE, U.K.

© 1999 by Beatrice Gormley
Published 1999 by
Eerdmans Books for Young Readers
an imprint of
Wm. B. Eerdmans Publishing Co.
255 Jefferson Ave. S.E., Grand Rapids, Michigan 49503 /
P.O. Box 163, Cambridge CB3 9PU U.K.

Printed in the United States of America

04 03 02 01 00 99   7 6 5 4 3 2

Library of Congress Cataloging-in-Publication Data

Gormley, Beatrice.
Miriam, written by Beatrice Gormley.
p.   cm.
Summary: While living in Pharaoh's palace in ancient Egypt,
Miriam, the sister of Moses in the Hebrew scriptures,
struggles to remain loyal to her people and her God.
ISBN 0-8028-5156-8 (pbk.: alk. paper)
1. Miriam (Biblical figure) — Juvenile fiction.
[1. Miriam (Biblical figure) — Fiction.
2. Egypt — Civilization — To 332 B.C. — Fiction.
3. Bible stories — O.T. — Fiction.]
I. Title.
PZ7.G89355Mi   1999
[Fic] — dc21   98-17761
                                         CIP
                                          AC

To my daughters, Katie and Jen

Contents

The Setting for Miriam's Story

By the time of Rameses the Great of Egypt (about 1304-1237 B.C.), the Hebrews have been living in Goshen, in the Eastern Delta of the Nile River, for hundreds of years. But they have not merged into the Egyptian population, partly because of Egyptian prejudice against foreigners and partly because of the Hebrews' loyalty to their own culture and religion. Miriam's clan, the Levites, are especially faithful Hebrews.

Originally the Hebrews were given land of their own in the Delta to farm. But their rights have eroded, until now they are poor tenant farmers and forced laborers on Pharaoh's many construction projects.

In the politics of the Egyptian empire, there is an ongoing struggle between Pharaoh and the priesthood of Amon-Re, centered at Thebes. Rameses the Great has deliberately moved his capital down the Nile from Thebes to the new city of Pi-Rameses, in the Eastern Delta, to escape the priests' influence. The Thebans, in turn, seek to control Pharaoh by stirring up Egyptians' fear and hostility toward Easterners — chiefly, the Hebrews. Just before the story opens, the government of Egypt has issued an edict meant to appease the Theban priests. It is an edict against the Hebrews.

Note: Within this book, some of the chapters are told from the viewpoint of Miriam, the main character, and some from the viewpoint of Nebet, the chief lady-in-waiting of Egyptian princess Bint-Anath. The chapters from Miriam's viewpoint will feature her name in Hebrew on the chapter title page: מרים. The chapters from Nebet's viewpoint will feature her name in Egyptian hieroglyphics: ⏛𓏤.

CHAPTER 1

The Promise

מרים

The first time I sensed my special gift, I did not even know it was special. I certainly did not guess it was the same gift as our ancestor Joseph's. My mind was not on myself at all, for it was the evening of my brother Aaron's weaning celebration. I was proud of my bright, healthy little brother, proud of my family, and looking forward to an evening of songs and stories.

As I waited at the bottom of the ladder, I hitched Aaron up on my hip. The air was hot and stale in the shadows between our hut and Uncle Hebron's, but there would be a breeze on the rooftop. I watched the members of my family climb the ladder to the roof, turning into black outlines against the western sky.

First went *Abba* — my father, Amram. He reached down a lean, muscled arm to pull up my grandfather,

Kohath. *Sabba* (Grandfather), as the whole clan called him, was so stiff in the joints that it was hard for him even to climb the ladder. Next came Imma (my mother, Jochabed) balancing a small jug of wine on her head. Finally I, Miriam — the family calls me Miri — climbed the ladder with Aaron clinging to my neck.

On the roof next door, Uncle Hebron and Aunt Shiphrah and my five cousins were already enjoying the fresh air. Ephraim, my oldest cousin and almost a man, was asking his father something about the sheep flock. Tamar, the next oldest, was lighting their oil lamps.

Tamar was thirteen, a year and a half older than I was, but we were close. Every day of my life, as far back as I could remember, she had greeeted me the same way she did now. "*Shalom*, peace, Miri." A smile broke out on her round face, and she looked glad to see me, although she had already seen me more than once today.

"*Shalom*, Tamar." I smiled back; she always made me glad to see her, too.

The flat rooftops of the clan of Levi were so close together that a grown person could step across from one roof to the other. And tonight all the families were up on their roofs, waiting respectfully for the ceremony to start.

Next to Uncle Hebron and Aunt Shiphrah's hut was that of my grandfather's nephew, with his second wife and eight children (two from his first marriage) and his widowed mother. Behind my aunt and uncle's, and partly behind our hut, was the home of my grandfather's younger cousin, with his wife and their five girls and the two orphan boys (distant relatives) they had adopted. And so on. Each rooftop was full of people linked somehow or other to all the rest of the clan.

In the almost-darkness their lamps made pools of yellow light, picking out the Hebrew section of the village. The Egyptians would be up on their rooftops, too, to catch the evening breeze. But this was not their celebration, and so they would not waste precious oil by lighting their lamps.

Beyond our village, the flooded fields spread out in every direction. The western horizon, on the other side of the river, was a black line against the setting sun. Just above it hung the crescent of the new moon. In the east, the sky had already turned dark blue, and the flat horizon was almost invisible.

Sabba, as head of our family, led the ceremony. Taking Aaron from me, he lifted him up. In his deep, mellow voice that carried across the rooftops, he said, "Praise God, who has brought our Aaron safely from infancy to childhood!"

"Praise God," we all repeated. From other rooftops of the Hebrew quarter, voices echoed, "Praise God."

I wondered if other people were feeling, as I was, a bit of sadness underneath the joy. There were so many children who had not survived. Aunt Shiphrah's sixth child, a little girl, had died of floodtime fever. Thinking of this and other dangers as *Sabba* handed my little brother back to me, I gave Aaron a squeeze and a kiss on the top of his curly head.

Our family sang the hymn of thanksgiving for the weaning of a child, and then the wine jug was passed around the rooftops. Each person took just a small sip, of course. Wine was expensive, only for special occasions. In my opinion, one sip was plenty, anyway.

"Congratulations," the other Hebrews called out to our family. I sat down against the low wall surrounding the roof and settled Aaron, drowsy and limp, on my lap. I closed my eyes and savored the glow that the tangy, sweet wine made in my throat.

"Huh," grunted *Sabba*, rubbing his shoulders from the effort of lifting Aaron. "In the old days, when my grandfather was head of the family and we celebrated my brother's weaning, we feasted the whole clan with roast kid. And we drank more than a sip of wine apiece, I can tell you that."

My father sighed loudly. Maybe he was only weary from his day in the brickyards. Or maybe he would rather not hear any more about how good life used to be in the old days.

Aunt Shiphrah leaned over the low wall of her roof. A tear gleamed on her round cheek — she, too, must have been thinking of her lost baby. But my aunt loved celebrations, and she was smiling eagerly at my grandfather. "*Sabba*, tell us a story. About the *old* old days, before we came to Egypt."

"Yes, a story, please, *Sabba!*" The families on neighboring rooftops quieted and drew as close as they could to listen. My grandfather cleared his throat.

"Many years before our clan came to Egypt, our

ancestor Abraham and his wife Sarah" — the people listening murmured appreciatively, because this was one of our favorite stories — "lived far across the Great Eastern Desert, in the land of Canaan. Now Abraham and Sarah were old, very old — almost twice as old as I am."

That was hard for me to imagine. *Sabba* was the oldest person in the clan, although there was an Egyptian woman in the village who was supposed to be older.

"And to their sorrow," my grandfather went on, "though they had flocks of fine sheep and goats, they had no children."

A sympathetic hum ran across the rooftops. No children! Could any misfortune be worse than to grow older and older, and finally to die, with no children or grandchildren to come after?

"One day, the Lord God spoke to Abraham."

God spoke. What was it like, to listen to God? Once I had asked *Sabba*, but he had only frowned into the distance and shaken his head. That was not a question to ask, or a question to be answered.

"God told Abraham," my grandfather went on as the sliver of new moon sank out of sight in the west, "that his aged wife, Sarah, would bear a son. And not only that. Because Abraham had been faithful, God promised that his descendants would be as many as the stars in the heavens."

As *Sabba* spoke, the last of the blank blue daylight melted away. I caught my breath.

Of course, I had heard this story about Abraham

7

many times, and I had seen the stars every night of my life. But never had the words of the story and the sight of the stars come together for me like this.

I saw — I saw what God had shown Abraham. "*This* many descendants," God told our ancestor, and He pointed to the glittering heavens.

I was no longer aware of Aaron's weight on my lap. I forgot about the fields and the village and the people on the rooftops. I was floating among the dazzling stars. I was dizzy with delight, God's delight in the stars — and in us.

I felt so close to the Power at the center of all things that I should have been terrified. I should have died of fear.

Instead, I was alive with joy.

CHAPTER 2

A Decree from the Palace

מרים

I could have floated there for a heartbeat, or for a year. I do not know how much time passed before I became aware of a silence. There was a fearful mood underneath it, and it seemed to pull me back down to earth. I felt off balance now, as if I had gone away from my village and then come back to find it changed. A pulse seemed to beat behind my eyes.

My grandfather had stopped talking. At first I wondered if he was pausing to let us think about God's glorious promise to Abraham. But then I noticed the anxious frown on my mother's face, and I realized that everyone was listening to something besides *Sabba's* story. The ladder was creaking.

"Who's there?" called my father.

A man's head and shoulders appeared above the wall. Although the light of the oil lamp did not reach

9

his face, I knew instantly that he was an Egyptian, because his hair was short. But he was not one of our neighbors, because his shoulders were too fleshy for him to be a hard-working tenant farmer. Besides, copper beads gleamed in the collar on his chest. It must be Peneb, the steward of the landlord's estate.

"A celebration going on up here, hm?" said Peneb. He spoke Hebrew, although with an Egyptian accent, in a loud, slurred voice. "Nobody invited *me*."

I was sitting close to the ladder, and I had to turn my face away from the stale beer on his breath. Aunt Shiphrah muttered, "I think he has already had his own celebration." My mother whispered bitterly, "He cannot leave us alone, even at night!"

"Sh!" warned Uncle Hebron. He was the leader of the clan council, so he was the man who dealt with the steward for us. "Sir," he called to Peneb, "we are only poor farmers, but we hope you will honor us by sharing in our celebration." Stepping over the wall of our roof, he picked up the jug and offered it to the steward.

Peneb, still on the ladder, leaned his elbows on the wall as he drained the jug. He wiped his mouth with the back of his hand and belched. "Well, what is it you are celebrating? One of your peculiar little Hebrew festivals?"

"My son's weaning," my father spoke up. I shivered at the note of anger in his voice. My father did not get angry easily, but when he did, it was hard to calm him down. Did Steward Peneb not realize how easily a man on the rooftop could push the ladder

away from the wall, sending a man on the ladder top-
pling to the ground?

But Uncle Hebron put a steadying hand on my father's shoulder, and Peneb did not seem to notice anything wrong. "Very nice," said the steward in a kindly
tone. "Congratulations. Oh — that reminds me. I
have an an-announcement" — he stumbled over the
word — "for the Hebrews in the village. Attention, all
you Hebrews!"

As if he needed to command our attention now! The
steward, acting for the landlord, ruled our lives. Each
year the clan council had to humbly beg him to allow us
to travel to the pastures for the shearing festival. When
my grandfather became too sore in the joints to haul
baskets of clay in the brickyards, Peneb had generously
excused him from duty on Pharaoh's work gangs — as
long as *Sabba* brought him gifts now and then. Peneb did
not instruct the scribes to tax the vegetables we grew on
our little private plots — he was satisfied with taking our
best melons and lettuces for himself.

Of course we listened to what he said, even when
he was half drunk.

"A new decree just arrived from the palace," Peneb
continued. "The palace" meant Pharaoh, who ruled
the Delta and all the rest of Egypt from his palace in
Pi-Rameses. "Yes, a new decree," Peneb went on. He
belched. "No more boys for you Hebrews."

No more boys? There were gasps from the people
on the rooftops, and my mother seized Aaron from
my lap. At the same time, my father moved in front of
his wife and son with his fists clenched.

11

A clamor rose among the clan. Was it a joke? Had they heard wrong? No more boys! What did the decree mean?

"No more male babies to be born to Hebrews," said Peneb. "At least that is what the decree says, by order of Pharaoh's (may he live and prosper) Minister for Foreign Residents. Now, do not take this too much to heart. These decrees are not always enforced. Half of them are simply the result of officials in the palace decreeing at each other, so to speak. But it is always wise to be careful. You — is that you there, Shiphrah?" He pointed to my aunt. "You and the other midwife will have to take care of it. . . . I suppose there is no more wine?"

"If only there were," said *Sabba*, "it would all be yours. It is my family's sorrow that we cannot offer to you, respected sir, a whole storehouse of wine jars — no, a whole canal full of wine."

I wondered whether Peneb would notice the edge of sarcasm in my grandfather's voice. But the steward only grunted, "I guess that fancy language means, 'no more wine.'" The ladder creaked as he climbed down; he belched again, and was gone.

A rising babble ran around the rooftops. "What did he mean?" "It is inhuman, impossible!" "He was drunk; you cannot believe him." "Could it possibly be true? It makes no sense! How can we keep on laboring in the brickyards for Pharaoh if he will not allow any more boys to grow up?"

And right next to me, *Sabba*'s voice, low and fierce: "How long, O Lord, before you send us a second Joseph?"

"Enough for tonight," called Uncle Hebron. "It is too late. But tomorrow night, all heads of families come to my rooftop. We will discuss the matter then."

As the neighbors began to climb down from the rooftops, Aunt Shiphrah reached over to my mother. "That pig Steward Peneb certainly knows how to spoil a celebration!"

Imma, holding my sleeping brother over her shoulder, smiled and freed one hand to squeeze Shiphrah's. "Never mind. I have my little lamb; that is all that matters."

I lingered on the rooftop, waiting until the others were down to put our lamp out. I was still dazed from what I had seen and felt while *Sabba* was telling his story. Catching my cousin Tamar's eye, I said, "At least we saw God's promise. And was it not glorious, floating among the stars, before the steward interrupted?"

Tamar smiled at me in a puzzled way. "We *heard* God's promise, you mean. . . . 'Floating among the stars'? What are you talking about?"

I shrugged and pinched out the lamp, suddenly confused. I gazed up at the sky again. Now the stars seemed so far from me and my clan that I almost cried out. There was God's promise, but what was the connection between God's care for us and the way Pharaoh treated us like farm animals? I could not even hold both those things in my mind at the same time.

"Well, then. *Shalom*, peace, Miri." Tamar's voice floated over to me in the dark.

13

But my head throbbed, and peace was not what I felt.

CHAPTER 3

A Difficult Princess

As the sky-goddess Nut prepared to give birth to the sun, the stars faded overhead. A woman past youth, but by no means aged, strode along the tile-floored galleries of the palace. Her shoulder-length wig was curled in the current fashion, but it was not so long or elaborate as to get in her way. She wore a plain but crisply pleated linen robe, and her simple but costly jewelry showed her importance. Nebet, chief lady-in-waiting to Princess Bint-Anath, was already up and at work as usual.

The princess would not rise until an hour or so after dawn, but many preparations for her day had to be made in advance. Bint-Anath expected Nebet to personally arrange all the details of her life, but she also expected Nebet to attend her constantly. This was unreasonable — but Princess Bint-Anath, beloved daughter of King Rameses the Great (may he live and prosper), was not required to be reasonable. Therefore, Nebet had to do much of her arranging while the princess was asleep.

This morning, Nebet stopped first at the tradesmen's courtyard, to interview a Mycenaean merchant. He spread out sample wares on a mat for Nebet to inspect. "See, lady — all the very finest merchandise from the Land of Punt. Note the craftsmanship of these ivory figurines, the heavenly scent of these sandalwood boxes — and look at these silk balls!" He handed her a bright red-and-yellow ball the size of a pomegranate. The covering was shiny, but also soft. "A toy fit for a royal baby, hm?"

Nebet let the ball drop to the mat as if it had burned her. "You may come this afternoon to the princess's lesser reception courtyard," she told him coldly, "on the other side of the colonnade from where the new guest quarters are being built. Display the ivory and sandalwood, but do not show these balls. Do not even bring them if you wish to trade in Pi-Rameses again."

Leaving the merchant bowing and stammering, Nebet strode off in the direction of the cookhouses. What a fool. If *she* were a merchant calling on the palace, she would never go in so unprepared. She would arrive the day before with a special gift for a servant who could furnish her with essential information.

For instance, that the Princess Bint-Anath was childless.

On her way to select a fowl for the princess's dinner, Nebet was slowed down by a large group crossing her path. Guards with Theban helmets were followed by several priests, and last, the High Priest of Amon, a lean man with an air of power. He must be returning from the sunrise prayers. Like the others in his path, Nebet drew aside, bowed deeply, and waited for him to pass.

There were many, many gods in Egypt. Most of them were local gods, of little importance outside their own towns. Certainly not so important that Lady Nebet should bow to their priests. But Amon was not only the deity of Thebes, the greatest city in Upper and Lower Egypt. He was also Amon-Re, the sun god, who made the crops flourish and gave light and life to all. Thus the High Priest of Amon was — aside from Pharaoh himself — the most powerful man in the kingdom.

The High Priest had arrived from Thebes a week ago, but Nebet had not yet found out why he was here. Not the official reason — the real reason. It probably had nothing to do with Princess Bint-Anath and her people, but still . . . it might be useful to know.

Raising her head, for an instant Nebet looked right into the priest's pale crocodile eyes. As if in awe, she dropped her gaze. But she was thinking, Of course, the High Priest does not have as much power here as he does at home in Thebes.

No need to let the High Priest know that Nebet, lady-in-waiting to Princess Bint-Anath, had some power of her own. She would instruct one of her informers, a wigmaker, to strike up an acquaintance with the barber who shaved the High Priest every day.

After the High Priest and his train were a safe distance away, Nebet went on to the cookhouse and picked out a plump pigeon. On the way back to the royal apartments, she paused by the stable-yard and waved to a young officer-in-training. He smiled briefly from his chariot, intent on aiming his arrow at the target. That was her younger son, Inyotef, so like his father.

Both boys, brought up by Nebet's brother after her husband died, were well on their way to promising military careers. Nebet was proud of them, but at this point, they were really more like nephews than sons. She had no daughter, and although she was not quite past childbearing age, she had decided not to remarry.

On to the music-master's courtyard, where Nebet had a word with him about the entertainment for the princess's next party. Finally she returned to the princess's suite just as Bint-Anath was opening her lovely almond-shaped eyes.

Speaking aloud, even in private, Nebet would never dream of referring to the princess without her title. She was always "Princess Bint-Anath," or "the princess," or "her highness." But in the secret chamber of her own mind, Nebet felt free to think of the princess as "Bint-Anath" without any title, as if she were Nebet's daughter or niece.

Nebet clapped for the servants to bring bread and fruit, and summoned the other ladies-in-waiting to help her highness prepare for the day. While the princess was being bathed and dressed, Nebet went over the day's schedule. She was never sure that Bint-Anath was really listening — in the middle of Nebet's explanation of the guest list for the Queen's banquet that evening, the princess began teasing her pet monkey by flicking water at it. The monkey started to leap around the room, knocking over cosmetics jars and jewelry trays and scolding loudly.

"Your duck pendant!" exclaimed Nebet, spotting an exquisite gold necklace swinging from the monkey's paw. "The King (may he live and prosper) had that pendant made especially for you! He presented it to you at the dedication of the great statue on the riverbank, where your image stands at the knee of his image! May I remind you — "

"What were you saying about the Assyrian delegation, Nebet dear?" Trying to stop laughing, the princess caught the excited monkey and petted him. "Chi-Chi, I was only teasing! I *love* my little monkey. There, there."

Nebet, pressing her lips together, pried the pendant from the monkey's paw. She handed the necklace to another lady, who reverently replaced it in its ebony tray. The princess flashed Nebet a naughty smile. "I know you will take care of everything, so why should I worry about it?"

"There are limits, Princess," said Nebet stiffly, "to what I can 'take care of.' Promise me that you will not take your parrot to the Queen's banquet."

"My parrot?" The princess set the monkey down near a bowl of fruit and held out her arms so the maids could dress her. She tried to look innocent, but a wicked chuckle escaped her throat. "But everyone was so entertained by him at that tedious reception. My father the King (may he live and prosper) was greatly amused at what the parrot said about the Grand Vizier."

"But the Grand Vizier was not amused," Nebet reminded her. Bint-Anath was intelligent, but she had no common sense — and apparently no political sense, either. She thought that because she was the King's favorite daughter, she did not need to worry about making enemies. In some ways, Princess Bint-Anath acted like a spoiled little girl, although she was not much younger than Nebet. If she would spend less time absorbed in herself and more time paying attention to palace politics, she would realize that the vizier was not a good enemy to have. She would also realize that she had a duty to her ladies and servants, because her enemies would have to be their enemies, too.

Breaking free of the maid who was pinning her robe, Princess Bint-Anath seized Nebet by the shoulders and kissed her on both cheeks. "Dear Nebet, do not look so grim! What would I do without you? My own mother has given up on me." She said the last words in a choked voice, and Nebet could not help embracing her.

It was true: the royal wife Ystnefert seemed to have lost interest in her own daughter. At first, when Bint-Anath failed to get pregnant, Ystnefert had done everything she could think of to help. She had presented expensive offerings to Osiris, god of fertility, and Hathor, Queen of Heaven and the official goddess of childbirth; she had consulted the best astrologers; she had searched the empire for the most learned physicians. But when Princess Bint-Anath remained childless, the Queen had firmly turned her attention to her son, Mer-en-Ptah. Nebet could not really blame her — most likely he would inherit the throne.

For her part, Nebet had tried to get the spirit of her dead husband to intercede for the princess. Of course he had not succeeded. He had always been a steady man and a good provider, but he had had no sense of politics when he was alive — why should he now, as a spirit? It was time to try something else.

CHAPTER 4

A Bargain with Taweret

After the noon meal, Nebet rested only briefly. The midday heat was still shimmering in the courtyards when she filled a basket with flowers and fruit. Through colonnades and gardens, past construction sites and storehouses, she made her way to a neglected corner of the palace grounds. Most of the ladies-in-waiting would not even know that there was a shrine behind the thorn hedge beyond this compost heap, or think it was important if they did. But Nebet knew that what people did when they were desperate was always important.

The shrine, set into a niche in the hedge, framed a small statue of an upright female hippopotamus. It was a measure of Nebet's devotion to Princess Bint-Anath that she had put aside her pride as a noble-woman to visit this shrine. Taweret, protector of pregnant women, was not dignified and beautiful like Hathor, Queen of Heaven. Of course, Hathor was identified with the cow, but only by her gracefully curved horns. In contrast, Taweret looked silly, with her hippo ears sticking out of her long wig and her little piggish eyes outlined with kohl. But with her swollen belly and heavy breasts, she was pregnant, as clearly pregnant as a female could be.

Besides, Nebet mused, one's official position did not necessarily reflect one's actual power. Taweret might rank far below Hathor in the hierarchy of the gods, but she had important connections. For instance, as a river animal, she was close to Osiris, who caused the yearly life-giving floods of the Nile.

Someone else had recently visited the shrine, because there were honey cakes at the goddess's feet and flies buzzing around them. Nebet scooped up the cakes and their flies, which might annoy a hippopotamus, and threw them over the hedge, onto the compost heap. Then she hung a wreath of lotus blossoms around the goddess's thick neck, where their perfume would rise into her nostrils. She arranged pomegranates and fresh figs on fig leaves in front of her feet.

"See, O Mother Taweret!" Nebet bowed deeply before the shrine. "The sweetest-scented flowers, the juiciest pomegranates, the most succulent figs from the garden of her highness, Princess Bint-Anath. This is only a little taste of what you can expect if her dearest wish is granted. I think I can promise you a shrine right in her garden — perhaps even a temple of your own."

There. That ought to get the attention of this peasants' goddess.

THAT AFTERNOON, after viewing the Mycenaean merchant's wares, the princess and her ladies relaxed in her private garden, as usual. Nebet was not one to sit popping honeyed dates into her mouth and chatting idly, or to toss crumbs of cake to the ducks on the pool, or even to play the board games to which some ladies were devoted. But she made use of her time in the garden by collecting bits of information from ladies or servants, or dropping a hint or two in the right ears.

At the end of the day, Nebet supervised Princess Bint-Anath's dressing for dinner. Her finest linen robe was ready, with all its perfectly ironed pleats. The hairdresser settled a perfectly fitting wig on the princess's shapely head and arranged the rippling locks, one by one, with an ivory hairpin. A maid fastened on the jewelry Nebet had laid out. The pieces were splendid, but not quite as splendid as the jewelry Nebet knew (because she had checked with Queen Ystnefert's head lady-in-waiting) that the Queen would be wearing.

By the time Bint-Anath left for the Queen's banquet in a train of guards and slaves with torches, Nebet was weary. She glanced longingly at her bed, outside the princess's chamber, but sleep would have to wait. She still had a meeting with her informer the wigmaker.

The wigmaker was waiting for Nebet in the princess's garden. As she seated herself on a bench, he crouched in front of her. "I did speak with the High Priest's barber," he said. "He was glad to be offered wine, since the priests abstain."

"Yes?" prompted Nebet.

"He thinks the High Priest still hopes to have the capital returned from Pi-Rameses to Thebes. The priests of Amon-Re are trying to spread the idea that the Eastern Delta is not the proper place for the Pharaoh's main residence. They are dropping a word here, a word there about how many immigrants from the East there are around Pi-Rameses."

"Immigrants?" asked Nebet in surprise.

"Well, I suppose he means groups like the Canaanites and the Hebrews," explained the wig-maker. "It is true that they have been in the Delta for generations, but some of the Egyptian workers resent them."

Ah. Something fell into place in Nebet's mind, like one of the interlocking pieces of a cleverly carved puzzle the princess had given her. Another source of hers, a scribe in the Ministry of Foreign Residents, had told her about a new decree the other day. A decree forbidding Hebrews to have male babies.

Nebet had assumed that the landowners in the Western Delta, who had no Hebrews on their estates, were behind that decree. It was rumored that the Western nobles thought it was unfair for the Eastern nobles to fill their work-crew quotas with unpaid Hebrews, while they had to furnish Egyptian peasants to labor on Pharaoh's building projects.

But it seemed the matter was more complicated than that. This could be important information.

With a gracious smile, Nebet presented the wigmaker with a small bar of silver. "Well done, my good man."

"Why, thank you, lady!" He bowed and smiled and bowed, as if he had not expected to be paid. "It is always a pleasure to serve you."

CHAPTER 5

Pi-Rameses

מרים

Several days after the celebration for Aaron, I paddled the boat into town with my grandfather.

Yes! Me, Miri — not looking after my little brother, not helping *Imma* grind the barley, but gliding along the canal toward the river! And I was doing it not to get out of my chores, but to help the family.

At dawn, after my father left for his work-crew duty, my mother had said to my grandfather, "Going to town, *Sabba?*" She was just making conversation, because of course he was going to town. It was a market day in Pi-Rameses, and therefore a chance for Kohath the Storyteller to earn a hamper full of gifts.

But *Sabba* only groaned as he limped out of the hut. When *Imma* started to rub his sore shoulders, he waved her away. He chanted the morning hymn, but then he made no move to get ready for town.

A worried line creased *Imma's* forehead. She ducked into the hut and came out with my grandfather's best stole, the one he wore to market.

Sabba scowled, though he was usually gentle with my mother. "Do I *look* like I could haul a boat down to the canal and paddle it to town and haul it up on shore?" he snapped. "My joints feel like grindstones grating together."

Imma stood biting her lip and holding the blue-and-red patterned stole with tasseled ends, a fine piece of work that she had woven herself. It seemed that *Sabba* really was too stiff and sore to manage the boat by himself. For the first time in years, then, he would not make his weekly trip to market. He would not return with the extra grain and oil that made the difference for us between hungry and full.

I followed my mother's gaze to Aaron, who had stooped to watch a beetle — he was the only one of us not worried. It seemed to me that my brother's backbone stuck out more sharply already. My own stomach growled, as if it were looking ahead to a disappointing supper tonight.

Then I had a brilliant idea. "What if *Sabba* had only to sit in the boat, while someone else did the work? *I* could paddle the boat and carry the hamper!"

Of course my mother's first thought was that it might be dangerous, or improper, or both, for me to accompany my grandfather to market. But *Sabba* gave me a long, measuring look (while I held my breath). Then he nodded, and motioned *Imma* to place the stole on his shoulders.

And now here I was in the stern of our pitch-covered reed boat, paddling toward the river. I knew how to handle the boat, for Tamar and I were allowed to use it now and then. We went fishing in the canal, or carried heaps of cut papyrus for basket-making from the marsh to the village. As I paddled, *Sabba* sat at ease in the bow, the tassled ends of his stole fluttering in the breeze. Like a merchant with servants, he had nothing to do but shade his eyes and wave to the villagers.

He waved to Aunt Shiphrah, coming down to the canal to fill her water jar. She waved back — and then pointed at me, her eyes and mouth wide in a surprised grin. I could not take time to explain, but I knew she would approve. My aunt's favorite saying is, "Risk planting one seed, and reap the reward of a hundred." My mother does not have my aunt's sense of adventure. *Her* favorite saying is, "Old ways are best."

My grandfather once remarked that I took after my aunt. He was only joking, of course, because she is not a blood relation. But I saw what he meant, and I felt proud — until I noticed the hurt expression on *Imma's* face.

Still, I could not help being glad that I was risking this trip to the city. I had never been to Pi-Rameses before, although I had lived within sight of its towers all my ten years. I had hardly been out of the village, Demy-en-Osiris, except to the yearly sheep-shearing festival at the edge of the Great Eastern Desert. Since my older sister Leah had married and gone to live in the landlord's household, I had been to visit her only once.

Now the thought of the city ahead gave me extra energy. I paddled past boys fishing with nets, goats grazing on the canal bank, and ducks dabbling among the tips of new reeds. The floodwaters had reached their highest point two weeks ago, and the first green shoots were springing up at the edge of the shrinking canal.

What a day! I wished I could spread the excitement out over days, not hours. I was not only escaping my chores. I would be seeing the great city of Pi-Rameses for the first time, *and* spending the day listening to *Sabba's* stories. I wondered if he would tell my favorite, the story of our ancestor Joseph.

I imagined Joseph as much like my Uncle Hebron, kind and calm. Except that Prince Joseph must have been taller and handsomer, and he would have dressed like a wealthy Egyptian, in a pleated kilt of fine linen and a gold-and-turquoise collar. And if Prince Joseph met Steward Peneb, he would not have to bow to the landlord's steward. No, Prince Joseph would watch Peneb bow to *him*.

Of course the beginning of the story of Prince Joseph was so horrible that I could hardly stand to listen to it. Joseph's own brothers sold him into slavery. And then they told their father that he had been killed by a wild beast. True, they were only Joseph's half-brothers, and true, Joseph had acted arrogant and overbearing — but still!

I thought of my brother Aaron, the way he listened so closely to me and repeated the words I taught him. And the way he put out his arms for "Miwi" to pick him up. I could not imagine being really angry with him, let alone selling him into slavery.

BY THE TIME we reached the river, my arms were beginning to ache with the unaccustomed paddling. I was glad to push the boat through the tufts of last year's papyrus and let it be drawn into the Nile's current. But I quickly realized that I could not just let the boat drift downstream. The river was as crowded as a sheep pen, and I had to work hard to steer out of the way of ferries and barges and galleys and flocks of reed boats.

The marshy edge of the river soon turned into a solid bank. Every bend in the river revealed some wonder, and I could hardly pay attention to the traffic on the water. Here came temple after temple, with great stone pillars and gold-covered doors and images of animal-headed gods. Here came the palace — not just a building but a whole town in itself, hidden by walls and protected by guard towers. And in front of the palace gates loomed a statue, threateningly tall in spite of the fact that it was seated. I stared, drawing in my breath sharply.

"Yes, that statue is large," said my grandfather dryly. "But Pharaoh himself is only a man, not a god as the Egyptians believe."

I still stared, noticing the smaller statue of a beautiful girl leaning against Pharaoh's knee.

"Miri! Be careful!"

Sabba's warning made me jump, just in time to

avoid the lumber barge bearing down on us. The traffic upstream and downstream was swirling into one tangled knot in front of the city gates. To my relief, I did not have to steer through the knot; peasants were not allowed to use the public docks. *Sabba* directed me farther downstream to a shallow inlet, and I beached our reed boat with dozens like it.

We climbed the bank to the market, which was a whole village of booths and stalls and people and animals outside the gates. There was so much to see and hear and smell that I longed to look around, but my grandfather hustled me along. "We are late," he grumbled. "What if some juggler takes my usual place?"

His usual place, it turned out, was beside one of the huge pylons that framed the city gates. A woodworker, a tall, lanky Canaanite named Talmai, had a permanent stall there, and he seemed glad to see *Sabba*. "Put your mat right here, Grandfather Storyteller," he called. "Help me drum up some business!"

Before I finished unrolling *Sabba's* mat and placing the open hamper where he told me, the audience began to gather. They sat on their haunches in the space in front of my grandfather or on the base of the pylon. I knelt on the edge of the mat and stared at them.

There were Egyptians in white linen, men and women with kohl-painted eyes. There were some very dark-skinned people; I knew from *Sabba's* stories that they were Nubians from the south. And those men with tattoos and pointed beards must be Lybians from the west. Then there were people so strange-looking that I could not even guess where they were from, like one youth about my cousin Ephraim's age, with oiled ringlets and a cinched-in waist.

When there was a good crowd, my grandfather held up his hand for quiet. He began to speak in Egyptian. First he welcomed his audience and told them a short, funny story at no charge. Then people began to step forward, placing gifts in the hamper: loaves of fine wheaten bread with sesame seeds, a pot of goose fat, and earrings of lapis lazuli, that stone as blue as the sky.

Those who gave a gift could request a story, a particular kind of story if they liked. *Sabba* told first an animal fable, then a love story, then the tale of a merchant's travels in strange lands. Eventually he launched into stories of terrible disasters.

The crowd seemed to like the disaster stories best. After *Sabba* finished the story of how God destroyed the wicked city of Gomorrah with fire from the sky, a sigh ran around the audience. There was a pause, and then Talmai the woodworker laid a carved walking stick beside the hamper. "Tell the story of the Great Flood."

I had heard about our ancestor Noah and his ark many times, of course. I only half-listened as *Sabba* began, "Long, long ago, in a land where the crops were watered with rain from the sky instead of a flood from the river . . ."

When my cousin Tamar and I were younger, we sometimes played a game we called "Land of Our Ancestors." We heaped up piles of mud from the canal bank for mountains and scratched plowed fields in the miniature valleys and built tiny huts and sheepfolds. Then I would dip a handful of grass in the canal and shake "rain" on the fields.

". . . there lived a man named Noah," *Sabba* was saying.

From where I was sitting, I could watch the audience, but I could also study the paintings on the whitewashed surface of the pylon in back of my grandfather.

The picture right above *Sabba* showed Pharaoh in his gilded chariot, wearing his blue war crown. He smiled calmly as he drew his bow to send another arrow flying toward his enemies. Dead soldiers, their bodies pierced with arrows, littered the ground under his two rearing warhorses. Pharaoh was larger than life-size, but his enemies — Easterners, judging by their striped tunics — were little, to show how unimportant they were.

My grandfather's voice pulled me back into his story. I was surprised at how different it sounded in Egyptian. When he had told the story of Noah and the Great Flood to our clan, up on the rooftop in the dark, it had seemed comforting. I had felt the coziness of the ark, and the way the floodwater rocked it like a mother rocking her baby.

But today, as I listened to the Egyptian words and watched the tense faces of the strangers in the audience, the story sounded like a threat. *Sabba's* voice seemed to be urging us to imagine what it would be like if the Great Flood poured into the city of Pi-

Rameses. The river would overflow, covering first the docks and then the stone steps to the city gates. The water would surge through the marketplace.

"And still the heavens poured water," my grandfather was saying, "and the floodwaters continued to rise. Up around the tree trunks and the walls of houses — "

At that moment, the marketplace seemed to fade away, like stars before the rising sun. The noise of merchants hawking their wares and customers bargaining and animals braying and bleating died away, too. And the painting of Pharaoh in his chariot began to change.

CHAPTER 6

The Gift

מרים

The painting seemed to spread out and come to life, as if I were inside it. Only I seemed to be standing on a high place, watching floodwater lap the hooves of Pharaoh's horses.

" — around the horses' hooves," I shouted.

The marketplace seemed far away, but I heard faintly my grandfather urging me to sit down, to be quiet. I felt — just barely — his hand pulling on my arm. I had never disobeyed *Sabba* in my life, but now the only thing that seemed important was the scene before me.

In the painting-come-to-life, Pharaoh scowled and whipped the horses, but the wheels only dug deeper into the soft sand. A foaming wave broke over the low back of the chariot, soaking Pharaoh to his knees. Words poured out of me in a loud voice: "Still the water rose, rose up to Pharaoh's knees."

I could not move or turn my head. In the scene before me the horses thrashed, trying to swim in their harness. Water lapped against Pharaoh's chest, and the reflection of his broad gold collar shimmered on the water. I drew in deep lungfuls of air and forced them out, needing more than anything to tell what I saw. "Up to Pharaoh's collar!"

As if from a great distance, I heard the crowd muttering. ". . . possessed by a demon?" ". . . entertaining, but this is too much!"

My grandfather was pleading, "She is in a trance. She does not know what she says."

But I, still trapped in the eerily clear scene, saw the water reach Pharaoh's chin. Water covered the confident smile, the proud nose . . . and finally, the cobra rearing from the front of Pharaoh's crown. A trail of bubbles broke the surface.

"Drowned!" I wailed, as loudly as a paid mourner. Even as the last sound rushed out of my throat, I began to come out of my trance. I found myself on my feet, with one hand stretched out to command the audience's attention and one hand pointing to the painting. *Sabba* was no longer trying to pull me down, and there was a reckless light in his eyes.

"A flood so deep," my grandfather intoned, "these mighty gates would be completely drowned!"

I blinked. The painting was dry and bright, and Pharaoh gazed over the heads of his warhorses with calm, kohl-rimmed eyes. The only water I could see was a blue bit of the river through the market stalls.

My legs were shaking so that I could hardly stand up, and my head pounded.

People in the crowd cleared their throats in a warning way, and heads in the audience turned toward a priest who had not been there when the story began. But now *Sabba* was the heedless one. He waved a hand dramatically at the painting. "This magnificent historic painting of Pharaoh (may he live and prosper), washed out of sight by God's flood!"

The audience was silent, except for the sound of shifting feet. The priest, I saw with increasing horror, must be somebody important — a high priest. Although Egyptian priests, with their shaven heads and white loincloths, all looked alike to me, this one was flanked by younger priests and soldiers. He rapped out, "Of which god do you speak, old man?"

"Such words are blasphemy," he continued without waiting for an answer, "for Set, the Scourge of the Eastern Peoples, would never drown the image of his beloved descendant, Rameses the Great. Nor would Amon-Re, nor Osiris. And such words are also treason, for who would wish to even imagine such a calamity for our land? Only an enemy."

By the time the high priest finished speaking, *Sabba's* audience had melted away. Talmai the woodworker, the same man who had saved a place for us, started shouting. "How dare you speak blasphemy, old man? We want only Egyptian storytellers in Pi-Rameses!" He lifted a copper amulet of a bull from his chest and held it up so that the priests could see. "As for me and my family, we have always worshipped the Bull."

At the same time, my grandfather seized the walking stick and used it to struggle to his feet. I jumped up to fasten the hamper and roll up the mat. I thought that any moment the soldiers would charge at us and beat us, but the priests seemed satisfied with driving us away. As we pushed our way out of the market, I glanced over my shoulder and saw the high priest speaking to his scribe. The scribe made a note on his tablet.

Back in the boat, we both had to paddle against the current of the river. *Sabba* was at the bow and I was at the stern, both of us facing forward. We did not talk. Gradually my heart stopped tripping, and it began to sink into me that I had ruined market day. The hamper was only half full. Besides, we had left before *Sabba* could trade the gifts — luxuries — for the grain and oil we needed.

In disbelief, I went over and over the moment when I found myself on my feet, pointing to the painting of Pharaoh. I, interrupting my grandfather's story! I, demanding the attention of a whole crowd of strangers! How could I have acted that way?

As the boat slipped past the palace dock, I threw a glance at the statue of Pharaoh. The king was smiling calmly, and so was the girl at his knee, the princess. I had acted as if *I* were as important as that princess, daughter of the most powerful man in the world. I was so ashamed.

WHEN WE REACHED the quiet water of our canal, my grandfather set down his paddle with a groan and stiffly edged himself around. There was a serious expression on his face, and I was sure he was going to reproach me. In our family, everyone had to think of the others. The worst thing you could do was cause the family hardship because of a selfish or careless action.

"*Sabba*," I blurted, "please forgive me! It must have been the story — it made me see . . ."

My voice trailed away as he gave me an odd look, almost a smile. "My storytelling never yet made anyone see visions," he answered. "You saw Pharaoh drowning in God's flood, did you not? You almost made me see it."

Me, see a vision? A vision was a waking dream, sent by God. People in the old stories — Prince Joseph or Noah — might see visions, but not an ordinary girl like me. *Sabba* must be joking. I stared at him, confused.

But my grandfather was not joking. His lined face had a strange expression: he looked excited and proud, but at the same time, sorry for me. "It has been many years since anyone in the clan had the Gift," he said. "Some said my aunt, my father's sister — directly in the line from Prince Joseph — had it. And now you, Miriam."

"What is the — the — Gift?" I whispered. He had called me by my full name, which meant this was a solemn occasion.

"It is the gift of listening when God speaks to us,

40

of watching when God shows us something. It is as if you were the only one in the clan with eyes or ears. You must watch, and tell us what you see. You must listen, and tell us what you hear."

I gasped, for with his words, the memory of God's promise in the stars burst vividly into my mind. "Once before I saw — yes, I did see — in the stars, like Abraham — "

As *Sabba* listened, nodding, I told him what I had seen and felt the night of Aaron's celebration. At least, I tried to explain it. It seemed impossible to put into words. But my grandfather, unlike Tamar, had some idea of what I was trying to express. "It must indeed be the Gift," he said.

His words alarmed me. *Sabba* seemed to think that something like this would happen again. It had not occurred to me before that paying attention to God might be dangerous. Gazing into the heavens the other night, I had felt close to great power, but also great joy and blessing. But the power of God's flood in my vision — that had made me feel like a straw borne on the mighty Nile River. I shrank from the thought of being seized by that power again.

Also, I remembered hearing that *Sabba's* aunt had been a very odd person. Some people said she could find things that were lost, or tell the shepherds out in the pastures where to dig a well. Other people made fun of her for prophesying things that could not possibly happen — horrible things, like the Nile running with blood.

My grandfather said no more, and I was afraid to

ask. After this lofty talk of visions, I was relieved to get back to the shabby but familiar village and our humble, ordinary hut. Aunt Shiphrah was sitting outside the door talking to *Imma,* who was grinding the barley for supper. Aaron and Rachel, my youngest cousin, played in the dust.

Aunt Shiphrah seemed upset about something, but she broke off to greet us and ask how market day had gone. My grandfather nodded. "Miri will come to market with me every week."

He said nothing about my vision or the priest, and *Imma* and my aunt did not seem to notice that we were home early. *Sabba* took a string of dried figs out of the hamper and gave us each one.

We were all silent, reverently tasting the almost unbearably sweet figs. They were a rare treat. Then Aunt Shiphrah took up the thread of her conversation again. "I do not blame *you,* Jochabed dear. I know you tried to bring Leah up right — but there she was, sitting at the loom with a Taweret amulet around her neck."

My mother looked unhappy. She murmured, "Maybe someone important at the villa gave it to her, and she feared she would offend them by not wearing it."

"Mm. She had no fear of offending *me,*" said Aunt Shiphrah dryly. "She did not even try to hide the amulet under her tunic. I said to her, 'Who do you think can give you a child — a clay hippopotamus, or the God of our ancestors?'"

My own sister, wearing an amulet of the Egyptian

goddess of pregnant women? I was not close to Leah the way I was close to my cousin Tamar, but I never would have expected her to show such disrespect for the ways of our people. This discovery about Leah was as disturbing, in a different way, as the discovery I had made about myself today. I remembered — as if it had been weeks ago — my excitement this morning, looking forward to going to Pi-Rameses with *Sabba*. Well, the day had been more exciting than I had bargained for. I felt strange new currents in my life, pushing as the river currents had pushed against our reed boat.

CHAPTER 7

Pharaoh's Daughter

מרים

For the next few days I waited to see how the Gift might show itself next. I listened more carefully to the words of the hymns and prayers, and I was amazed at how exactly some of the words described the way I had felt during my visions. And as I watched the scenes around me for signs that God was showing me something new, I was often full of wonder at ordinary things. Ripples of light on the water around a clump of reeds, or the smell of the newly plowed fields, could seem like a blessing.

But my life was full of other things, and I had no more visions at that time. Gradually I forgot to watch and listen, and I hardly thought about the Gift at all.

One afternoon, a month into the growing season, I was grinding grain outside our hut. My mother had been busy in the fields for weeks, help-ing my father sow the landlord's new barley and wheat. Now, while my father and Uncle Hebron and Ephraim dredged ditches and repaired the canal walls, *Imma* and Aunt Shiphrah were planting our leeks and garlic and lettuces and cucumbers and melons. We had a little plot, on a second-rate piece of land, where Steward Peneb allowed us to grow vegetables.

So besides looking after Aaron, and fetching reeds from the roof (where we dried them) for *Sabba*'s weav-ing, I was doing the daily grinding. My muscles were getting used to grinding grain, and my hands had cal-luses where I gripped the grindstone. Like *Imma*, I sang in time to the grinding, to make it less boring. *Imma* usually sang this song:

> *Man works from dawn to setting sun*
> *But woman's work is never done*
> *Thrum, thrum, thrum*
> *Thrum, thrum, thrum.*

I saw no point in singing about working while I worked. Scooping a handful of barley from the grain jar onto the grindstone, I started a song to take my mind off the chore:

> *Then Pharaoh said to our Joseph,*
> *"What could my dream mean?"*
> *And Joseph he said to Pharaoh,*
> *"Save from the fat years for the lean."*

Aaron liked my song; he danced back and forth in front of the grindstone with a funny little grin on his face.

Sabba sat nearby in the shade, pushing and tugging the reeds as he wove another pair of sandals. My song made him scowl, and I realized I had reminded him of one of his favorite subjects: how our clan used to have our own farms.

"Our ancestor Joseph gave his brothers the richest land in the Delta. The landlord's smaller northern wheat field — that was my *Abba's* own land. Yes, it was."

"Pretty," said Aaron, pointing to a daisy that I had tucked behind my ear.

"My *Abba* plowed his own land," *Sabba* went on, "and my *Imma* walked behind him, sowing their own grain. When the grain was ripe, the harvest was theirs. Of course they had to pay Pharaoh the grain tax," he admitted.

"Yes, pretty," I told Aaron as I scooped another handful of grain onto the grindstone. "Now say it in Egyptian." I reminded him of the Egyptian word for "pretty," and he repeated it with a lisp. "What a smart boy!"

"Pretty — mine," said Aaron in Egyptian, reaching for the flower. I had to laugh as I handed him the daisy. He tried to tuck it behind his own ear, and I laughed again.

Sabba was still talking about his boyhood. "In those days, there was no landlord's estate at the edge of the river, but a date-palm grove for the whole village. The trouble began when this Pharaoh's father came down from Thebes and built his summer palace in the Delta. Yes, that was the beginning. Our landlord's father was with that Pharaoh's court. One fine day — just like today, with a breeze blowing from the north — he drove his chariot into Demy-en-Osiris. Of course, it was not called 'Town of Osiris' then. No, our ancestors named our village 'Carmel' — 'God's fruitful field' — because the land was so fertile.

"Well, a troop of soldiers marched into the village behind the chariot. They gathered us farmers, mostly Hebrew then, and the landlord's scribe read from a scroll. The Pharaoh had deeded all the farmland to him."

My stomach clenched, and I bore down on the grinding stone with all my strength. I was beginning to understand why my father did not want to listen to *Sabba's* stories about the good old days. Those stories made you angry — so angry that you wanted to jump up and scream and push someone (Steward Peneb?) into the canal. Nothing good would come of that.

Just as I finished the day's grinding, Aunt Shiphrah appeared with a mattock over her shoulder. "Good day, *Sabba* Kohath. Did the ointment I gave you help your stiff knees? Miri," she said, handing me a small parcel, "I want you to take a message and this packet of herbs to your sister Leah at the villa. Go ahead," she added as I glanced at the barley meal. "I will start your porridge cooking before I go down to the vegetable beds. Tell Leah to steep these herbs overnight, then drink a cupful of the infusion every day from now until she gives birth."

Birth! My aunt must have gotten word that Leah was pregnant, then.

"And tell her we missed her at Aaron's celebration," growled *Sabba*. "Ask her if she is still Hebrew — or have she and that husband of hers turned into Egyptians?"

Scrambling to my feet, I took the packet of herbs and tucked it under my sash. Aunt Shiphrah must still be angry with Leah, or she would go to see her herself. But that was my good luck. "Come on, Aaron! We are going to the villa." I had to take him along, of course; *Sabba* could not run after him, and my aunt would stay at our hut only long enough to start the porridge. Still, it would be a small adventure.

IT WAS A long walk down the canal path to the river, and I ended up carrying Aaron most of the way. At the edge of the papyrus marsh, I turned and walked up the river the short distance to the villa. In this season, the marsh looked like a field of grain growing out into the water.

Where the walls of the villa grounds met the river, tall gates and a watchtower faced the landlord's dock. A large, brightly decorated barge with a striped awning was tied up at the stone steps. I noticed a royal cartouche — picture-writing inside an oval, which meant it was a royal name — under the prow. Someone from Pharaoh's palace must be visiting the landlord.

The sentries at the gates made fun of my Hebrew

accent when I explained my errand, but they let us in. I started toward the landlord's house with its pillared porch, intending to circle around to the weavers' quarters behind it.

"Halt!" one of the guards yelled after me. "Not the front door, peasant! Servants in back."

I bowed my head meekly and turned aside, down a lane of fruit trees. Inside, I was seething. Why did Egyptians talk to us like that, as if we were donkeys?

Out of sight of the guards, I was determined to take my time getting to the weavers' quarters, where Leah worked. I strolled through a stand of pomegranate trees, letting Aaron pat the brilliant red blossoms. In the distance, a row of stately date palms rose against the wall — had they once been part of our people's date grove?

As I came out of the pomegranate trees, my eyes were dazzled by the sun's reflection on a square pool, twice as large as the floor of our house. There was a grape arbor on this side of the pool, and flower beds on the other side.

"Quack!" said Aaron. He pointed to ducks calmly paddling among lotus leaves on the far side of the pool.

These must be tame ducks, I thought, because they paid no attention to us or to the gardeners working in a nearby flower bed. Breathing in the scent of lotus blossoms, I squinted across the pool. The gardener working the *shaduf,* the pole and bucket for raising water, looked like Leah's husband, but I could not be sure. I had seen him only once, at the wedding.

Aaron squirmed around in my arms and pointed over my shoulder. "Quack!" he said again.

I turned, thinking that he must have spotted a duck under the grape arbor. To my horror, I now noticed a woman sitting on the bench under the vines. Not just any woman — a lady in a white linen robe and splendid jewelry, including a gold pendant.

Dropping to my knees, still holding Aaron, I bowed my head. Why had I not gone straight back to the servants' quarters? Now I was in trouble. "I am sorry, lady," I stammered in Egyptian. "Sorry," chirped Aaron, as if I were teaching him another Egyptian word. He was staring at the lady. She looked somehow familiar to me. Was she one of the landlord's wives who appeared in public processions on feast days? But certainly I would have remembered such a beautiful lady.

I prayed the lady would understand that Aaron was only a little child and not take offense. I tried to pull him down into a bow. But he wiggled from my sweaty grasp and toddled toward the bench. "Pretty, pretty," he cooed, reaching out and wiggling his fingers.

As I was about to make a desperate lunge for Aaron, I heard the rustling of crisp linen behind me. I turned to see another woman, leading girls with trays. Her sharp glance took in the scene. In a dignified manner, she bowed to the lady on the bench. "These urchins must be annoying you, Pharaoh's daughter."

CHAPTER 8

An Unsuitable Child

When the rudder of the princess's barge broke, the captain recommended drifting back downriver to the palace docks to make the repairs. But at the very suggestion of giving up the day's outing, Princess Bint-Anath made a face like a child whose doll is taken away. If the princess sulked, there would be trouble for everyone around her. So Nebet had ordered the captain to pull into the nearest dock instead. The nearest dock happened to belong to Satepihu, a minor noble of the Eastern Delta.

Then Nebet had to go to Satepihu's chief wife, a gushy, fluttery person, and to indicate, in a tactful way, that the princess did not want to spend any time with her or her gushy, fluttery daughters. Only because her highness had such a headache, Nebet explained. However, the princess would graciously enter the villa garden, to wait in comfort while the barge was being repaired. Taking her cue, the landlord's wife quickly made the offer of refreshments.

Satisfied with the way she had arranged everything, Nebet led two of the villa slaves into the garden with trays of fruit and cold drinks. And then — horns of Hathor! Where had these grubby children come from?

The peasant girl on her knees before the princess — a Hebrew girl, judging by her striped tunic — looked frightened enough at first. But when Nebet said "Pharaoh's daughter," the lady-in-waiting thought the girl was going to faint. Then she recovered herself and was about to lunge for the little boy.

But Princess Bint-Anath lifted one slim, bejeweled hand. "No, let the child come."

"Pretty," said the boy. He pointed his grimy little forefinger up toward the princess's neck. For a Hebrew, he pronounced Egyptian words quite distinctly. "Mine."

At one sign from Princess Bint-Anath, Nebet would have ordered the slaves to throw these insolent beggar children off the villa grounds. But the princess laughed and held out her arms. The boy let himself be picked up, delighted (of course) to stand on the bench and finger her jewelry. Apparently it was not the rows of gold beads in the princess's collar that had caught his eye, but her gold duck pendant.

"Do you like the duck, little boy? I love ducks. That is why my father (may he live and prosper) had this made for me." Bint-Anath pushed the gold duck toward the boy, quacking, and he laughed and quacked back.

Seeing that the princess was determined to play with the peasant child, Nebet sent the slaves off to fetch towels and scent. At least she could play with a *clean* peasant child.

Then Nebet questioned the peasant girl — the little boy's sister, it seemed — and found that these children lived in one of Satepihu's villages, Demy-en-Osiris. They had come to visit their older sister, a weaver here at the villa.

Nebet dismissed the girl, telling her to go to the weavers' quarters. The girl obeyed, but glanced over her shoulder as she went. Quite a presumptuous peasant girl, thought Nebet, half amused. As if her brother might not be in good hands with the princess!

Watching Princess Bint-Anath play with the child, Nebet thought (as she had thought so many times before) how difficult her highness could be. The royal quarters of the palace were *swarming* with children: children of Pharaoh's wives, of his concubines, of his sons and daughters. In fact, Nebet had to go to a great deal of trouble to keep these children out of the princess's way, lest she fall into one of her black weeping moods.

If the princess wished, of course, she could play with any of those suitable palace children, any time she liked. She could even *adopt* a concubine's child; Nebet had tactfully suggested it once. Princess Bint-Anath had thrown an onyx vase at her head.

And now look at her highness, tickling this tenant

farmer's child to make him squeal! At least he was clean, thanks to a good scrubbing in the pool. He seemed bright for his age — or perhaps he was older than he looked. But many of the children in the palace were just as appealing. It was simply perverse of the princess to take up with a Hebrew child. By now, she knew as well as Nebet that the priests of Amon-Re were trying to use anti-Hebrew feeling against the King.

"Would you like some fruit, little boy?" the princess was saying. "Let us try a pomegranate!"

Taking the hint, Nebet cut a pomegranate into sections for them. Then she excused herself and went back to the dock to see what progress had been made in repairing the barge. To her relief, the boatmen had found an adequate rudder on the landlord's barge, and they had almost finished replacing the broken one.

By the time Nebet returned to the garden, the peasant child had managed to get pomegranate juice all over Princess Bint-Anath's fine linen robe as well as his own ragged tunic. His neck was wreathed with a string of pomegranate blossoms, presumably fashioned by her highness's own delicate hands.

Nebet was struck with a new worry: What if the princess took it into her head to bring the little boy back to the palace? What if the High Priest of Amon-Re heard rumors of a Hebrew child in the princess's suite?

Nebet tried to banish these alarming thoughts, lest she somehow plant an idea in the princess's mind that was not already there. She sent a slave to the weavers' quarters to summon the child's sister.

The princess was clearly sorry to part with her new playmate, but after many kisses, she handed the boy over to his sister. The Hebrew children left the villa behind Nebet and the princess, and the little boy waved to her from the dock as she blew him one last farewell kiss from the barge. That is the end of it, thanks be to Hathor, thought Nebet.

But when the villa was hidden by a bend in the river, something on the princess's neck caught Nebet's eye. Or rather, the lack of something. "Where is your gold pendant, your highness? It must have fallen off in the garden. We must go back to the villa and search for it."

Lounging under the striped awning, Princess Bint-Anath smiled regally at her head lady-in-waiting. "Calm yourself, Nebet dearest. You worry so much, you even worry about problems that do not exist. I did not wear that necklace today."

That was such a bold-faced lie that Nebet could only stare at her. When the princess smiled her blank smile, like the smile on her official statue, there was nothing more to say.

But there was plenty more for Nebet to think. The princess was getting increasingly reckless. It had been imprudent enough of her to offend the Grand Vizier. It was absolutely foolish of her to be seen playing with a Hebrew child, even though only on a minor nobleman's estate. But to lose her pendant and so risk losing her position as Pharaoh's favorite daughter — this was courting disaster indeed. Disaster for the princess — and for anyone connected with her.

CHAPTER 9

Quack

מרים

As I carried Aaron back down the canal path, he fed me from a section of pomegranate that he still held. He pushed the pomegranate seeds, like red jewels, into my mouth a few at a time. The juice was sweet and tart on my tongue, but my mind was buzzing with what had happened at the villa.

A princess, playing with my little brother! It was like falling into one of *Sabba's* more far-fetched tales. And, according to the gossip of Leah and her fellow weavers, this princess was Pharaoh's favorite. She was the girl — a woman now, of course — whose likeness stood beside her father's in the statue above the palace dock.

By the time we reached home, the afternoon shadows were long, and my mother and aunt were back from the vegetable garden. *Imma* caught Aaron up and kissed him — and then sniffed him. She was about to say something, but Aunt Shiphrah spoke first.

"Well?" she asked me, folding her arms. "How is your sister Leah?"

"She looks very healthy," I said truthfully. I had noticed that my sister's face had a rosy glow, and her hair was glossy. She had felt soft when I hugged her. I did not add that her eyes were lined with black kohl, like the eyes of the Egyptian women in the weavers' quarters.

As usual, my aunt could tell I was holding something back. "She was still wearing that Taweret amulet. Was she not?"

I nodded unhappily. That was the first thing I had noticed: the blue-glazed pendant of the hippopotamus goddess on a string around Leah's neck. "But she sends thanks for the herbs, Aunt Shiphrah. Truly — she was very glad to have them."

"Huh!" said my aunt.

Imma looked as if she wanted to ask something, but it was *Sabba* who spoke up next. "And why, pray tell, did not Lady Leah come to the celebration for her own brother Aaron?"

I lowered my head. I was ashamed of my sister, but since my grandfather asked directly, I had to tell him. "She said . . . she *was* going to come, but the landlord's wife was having a dinner party, and one of the serving girls was sick, and they wanted Leah to take her place . . ."

"I suppose she could not say no," suggested my mother.

57

I gazed at the hard-packed earth in front of the hut. I knew Leah had not tried to say no. She had explained to me what an honor it was for her to wait on the landlord's guests. But I did not want to betray her. "I guess they like her, at the villa," I said. "The housekeeper told Leah she had clever hands."

"The only clever part of her," said Shiphrah. "Oh, forgive me, Jochabed, but you know it is true."

Actually, I thought Leah was cleverer than my aunt guessed, but I was not going to tell her that. Leah had said something else about why she had not come to the celebration for Aaron: "It would not be wise for me to draw attention to being Hebrew, you know. There is talk against us. I have even heard Sir Satepihu scold Steward Peneb for letting Hebrews get away with this thing or the other."

It made me sick at heart to hear my sister talking like that. It was like a bad dream in which Leah had married not just into another clan, but into the landlord's estate. As if she had said to herself, I will not be a Hebrew anymore.

Suddenly I realized that I had an ideal excuse for changing the subject. "Oh! Wait till you hear about the princess!" I described how we had met Pharaoh's daughter in the garden, and how she had taken to Aaron.

"I wondered who had anointed you with expensive scent!" exclaimed my mother to Aaron. To Shiphrah she added, "Does he not look like a little prince, with a garland around his neck?" She lifted the string of wilted red flowers on Aaron's chest.

Aunt Shiphrah started to laugh, then gasped and stared. *Imma* followed her gaze, and the color drained from her face. *Sabba* muttered, "May the Lord save us!" From their horrified expressions, I thought there was a poisonous spider among the pomegranate blossoms.

But then I saw what frightened them so much: a pendant. The princess's gold duck gleamed against my brother's juice-stained tunic. "Quack!" said Aaron, delighted to see the shiny toy again.

AFTER MY FATHER and Uncle Hebron got home from the fields, and after we ate our evening porridge, the family held a council on the rooftops. The discussion went on for some time, since the adults could not agree on what to do with the gold pendant. *Imma*, still upset, wanted it thrown into the marsh. "It is an accursed heathen amulet, with which she seeks to bind my child to her!"

My father thought the problem was how to return the pendant to the princess without being accused of thievery. Aunt Shiphrah wanted to hide it and sell it to a trader at the next shearing festival. "That piece of gold would buy a whole flock of sheep," she pointed out. Uncle Hebron tended to agree with his wife, but he was worried about the danger to the clan if we kept the valuable pendant in our hut.

Nobody asked my opinion, of course, and I could not have explained it, anyway. It would have sounded as unreasonable as my mother's fears. But I had a feeling that the princess had meant to give the pendant to Aaron, and that we ought to honor her purpose and keep it.

Finally *Sabba* spoke. "The fact that none of us agree makes me think it is time . . . to call on Miriam's gift."

They all stared from my grandfather to me. "Our Miri has the *Gift!*" quavered my mother. My heart beat harder. I was proud, but also afraid of what would come next.

Sabba told them the story of what had happened in the market the first time I had accompanied him to town. "And so I believe," he concluded solemnly, "that this child Miriam has the gift of prophecy, a Gift like that given to our ancestor Joseph."

By now the full moon was up, and I could see the wondering expressions on my family's faces. My mother looked fearful as well. My own knees trembled as *Sabba* beckoned and I stepped forward.

Laying a hand on my head, my grandfather said a prayer. "Let this child have an open and waiting spirit this night. And if it be the Lord's will, give us guidance through her."

Then *Sabba* put his hands on my shoulders and looked into my eyes. "Understand, Miriam, that you must not try to decide for yourself what is best for the family to do. You must simply wait for whatever comes to you in your dreams tonight. And in the morning, tell me."

To end the council, *Sabba* led us in one of the evening hymns. As usual, he sang the verses, and we chanted the response after each verse. The response tonight was, "The children of men take refuge in the shadow of thy wings, O Lord."

THAT NIGHT, I dreamed I was down at the river, in the papyrus marsh. I was worried, because somehow Aaron had gotten out on the river by himself. He was floating on something — riding on a duck's back. At least, it was shaped like a duck, but its head and tail, the parts I could see, gleamed rich yellow.

Wait — that was not Aaron. It was a much younger child; in fact, I was amazed that he could hold onto the duck's back so well. But the most amazing thing was the feeling that came over me as I watched the baby. I felt a protecting presence in the golden glow around the little boy. From somewhere above me, I heard the words from the evening's hymn: "The children of men take refuge in the shadow of thy wings, O Lord."

THE NEXT MORNING my head ached, but I was glad, because I took it as assurance that the dream had come from the Gift. I hurried outside, where *Sabba* was chanting the hymn for daybreak, to tell him about my dream. He listened carefully, then nodded, as if he had gotten his answer. "It is well. We will keep the pendant."

After we ate our morning bread, and after *Imma* and *Abba* had left for the day's work, my grandfather directed me as I hid the pendant. Inside our hut to the right of the door, where the light from the smoke hole was faintest, I took a sharp stick and dug the mortar out from between two bricks. We put the gold duck into one of Aunt Shiphrah's small leather pouches, the kind she kept herbs in. Then I pushed the pouch deep between the bricks and sealed the space with moist clay. The new mortar dried before the end of the day. If I had not counted the bricks, I would not have been sure myself where the princess's pendant was hidden.

CHAPTER 10

Too Many Hebrews

In Princess Bint-Anath's suite of the royal quarters in the palace at Pi-Rameses, Nebet was supervising the packing. It was almost *akhet,* floodtime. Time for Pharaoh and his court to sail up the Nile to Thebes for the festival of the New Year.

Although the King traced his own ancestry to the god Set, he could not neglect the worship of Amon-Re. The New Year in Thebes, when the god Amon's image was brought from his temple and displayed to the people, was a national festival as well as a religious one. Wherever Pharaoh might be during the rest of the year, at the turning of the year he must be in Thebes. And so must his principal wives and his grown children.

Under Nebet's sharp eye, ladies and maids filled chests with the princess's shifts and robes and shawls. One special chest contained the paraphernalia she would need for the ceremonies, including her tall crown, with its horns representing the goddess Hathor, and her sistrum, the sacred instrument she shook as she danced. Smaller boxes were packed with her wigs, cosmetics, and jewelry.

As Nebet selected the necklaces, she tried to ignore a twinge of fear. The gold duck pendant was still missing. The King had not yet asked his daughter about it, but Nebet feared he would.

You would think, Nebet complained to herself, that with all his wives and concubines and sons and daughters, and all the gifts he presented to them on numerous occasions, this one piece of jewelry could slip his mind. But the King's mind was astonishing — not only when it came to matters of state, but also when it came to the particulars of his relationship with each person in his family. And since Princess Bint-Anath was one of his favorites, Nebet had the sinking feeling that he would remember the pendant.

The princess entered the bedchamber with a clinking of anklets, carrying her monkey. "Chi-Chi is so excited about our trip to Thebes, are you not, Chi-Chi? Nebet, do you think the High Priest would mind if he took part in the sacred dance?"

Nebet forced a laugh, as if to say of course Princess Bint-Anath was joking. "I thought the monkey would be more comfortable here at home," she said. "He hates water — do you not think he would be unhappy spending weeks on the boat?"

But even as she spoke, Nebet knew it was no use. Princess Bint-Anath's impish smile had vanished, leaving that remote, royal look on her face. Nebet bowed, making her own face blank. Never mind that she had spent weeks calculating the space in the princess's barge. Besides the princess and all her baggage, the barge must accommodate Nebet and four other ladies, the princess's hairdresser, and enough servants and slaves to make them all comfortable. Nebet would just have to figure out how to fit in Chi-Chi, as well as an extra slave to watch and clean up after the monkey.

At this prospect, Nebet felt a sharp twinge in her upper back. Perhaps she had been bowing too often.

TWO WEEKS LATER, the entire royal procession was strung out along the Nile at Thebes. Princess Bint-Anath's barge was near the head of the procession, and the princess herself was on display in full ceremonial garb. Shaking her sistrum, she led lesser princesses in a dignified sacred dance.

Nebet watched from a skiff, just within earshot of the shivery music of the sistrums. Besides her boatman, there was another passenger: Chi-Chi the monkey. Nebet kept a firm grip on his leash. No doubt the princess had only suggested including her monkey in the dance to Amon-Re to tease her head lady-in-waiting. But why take a chance? Besides, Nebet had another, more important reason to be away from the princess's barge at this moment.

From down the river, a barge glittering with gold leaf moved upstream to meet the royal procession.

That was the barge of Amon-Re, bearing the image of the god. The statue of Amon-Re, draped in gauze and framed in a gold box, was exhibited to the people only once a year, at this time. To catch a glimpse of it, they crowded the riverbank and thronged the water in boats.

Shading her eyes from the glare on the water, Nebet could make out two figures in front of the statue. One was Pharaoh, in his double crown and false goatee. The other, wearing the ceremonial leopard-skin as well as his usual white loincloth, was the High Priest of Amon-Re. Together they would offer the proper New Year sacrifices in full view of the people.

Nebet scanned the river again and spotted a skiff with a certain passenger — the one she had been looking for. She motioned her boatman to pull alongside. The scribe in the other skiff shot a puzzled glance at the monkey, but he bowed without comment. Nebet held up a hand in greeting. "What news have you, scribe?"

"The Ministry of Foreign Residents will issue two new decrees in due course, after our return to Pi-Rameses," he said. "First, foreigners from the East will no longer be allowed to own land in Upper and Lower Egypt."

Nebet smiled briefly. "They own no land now. The High Priest must know that is an empty gesture."

The scribe nodded. "My lady is astute in these matters. But they say the High Priest takes satisfaction even in maneuvering Pharaoh into making empty gestures. And the second decree will demand that all Hebrew male babies be killed at birth."

Absently Nebet yanked the monkey back from the prow of her skiff. She frowned as she said, "But I thought this same decree had been issued last *akhet*."

"Yes, but the legal difference between the wording of the two decrees is important," explained the scribe. "Last year's decree said to the landlords with Hebrew tenants (under its breath as it were), 'We want to *appear* to be controlling the Hebrew population, but you need not take the law seriously.' Whereas this year's decree says, 'We expect you to at least make a show of slaughtering a few Hebrew pups.'"

Nebet was silent, shuddering inwardly. What if Princess Bint-Anath had brought that Hebrew boy back to the palace? Of course he had been born even before the first decree — but still, there would have been trouble.

"I trust my lady is satisfied with my information?" asked the scribe in a politely reminding tone.

"Indeed," said Nebet. "Yes, quite satisfied." She handed him the jar of expensive perfume she had brought. He looked relieved, and she realized he must have been afraid she was going to present him with the monkey. Monkeys, which had to be imported from Nubia, were valuable, but (as Nebet knew) a great deal of trouble.

The lady-in-waiting and the scribe exchanged a few more polite words, and then the scribe's boatman steered off into the crowded river. Nebet turned her attention back to the ceremony. Now Princess Bint-

Anath was kneeling with her arms raised in homage to Amon-Re. The picture of regal dignity and piety.

When Bint-Anath decided to play her role, there was no woman in Upper and Lower Egypt better suited to be the ideal princess. It was moments like these that made Nebet most proud of Bint-Anath — her princess.

Nebet smiled fondly and shook her head.

CHAPTER 11

Bad News

מרים

In our village, another floodtime passed. One night during planting season, my sister Leah sent word that she was about to give birth. "Of course!" grumbled Aunt Shiphrah. "Just as I find a moment to rest after a hard day's work with the sowing." But she climbed wearily down from the rooftop to go to the villa and attend Leah.

I expected my aunt to take Tamar along as an assistant, which meant that I would have to look after my younger cousins as well as Aaron. Instead, Aunt Shiphrah chose me to bring along. "You have not yet seen a child come into the world, have you, Miri? About time that you did."

Leah had a healthy girl, thank the Lord, and my aunt praised me for my steadiness during the birth. "Not that it was difficult," Shiphrah added. "Leah takes after your mother — easy as a ewe dropping her lamb."

Still, I was proud that I had done well. As we walked home from the villa in the hour before dawn, I dared to say aloud what I had been hoping secretly. "Aunt Shiphrah, if you could train *me* to become a midwife — at least, as much training as you can give me, before I am betrothed — "

Aunt Shiphrah abruptly stopped walking and turned to face me. I could not see her expression in the dark, but I knew there was something wrong if my forthright aunt hesitated to speak. "Your mother has said nothing to you?" she asked finally.

I shook my head, more uneasy than before.

She began walking again. "Hm! Maybe I should not speak, either. *Sabba* Kohath has not yet decided what is best."

"Decided what?" Now I was wild to know, and I pleaded and hung on her arm until she explained.

"You have the Gift, Miri. I doubt that you should attempt to take on the calling of midwife as well. And as for marriage . . ."

I was shocked. Already dazed from the sleepless night, I wondered if I was dreaming.

"It is a heavy responsibility," Aunt Shiphrah went on. "Not just for you, but for the family — for the clan of Levi. We are not sure that you should be married out of the clan, or that you should marry at all. *Sabba* wonders if his aunt's Gift was damaged — not respected — when she was married and had to leave us for her husband's clan."

Not marry! That was unheard of, unless a girl was too feeble-minded or crippled to run a household. And I was already very capable. I could grind grain and make porridge or flatbread from the meal; I could bank a fire so that the coals stayed alive overnight; I could weave, although not as well as Leah or *Imma*. I had a way with little children, and I looked forward to the day when I would hold my own babies in my arms.

Tamar had been betrothed at the last shearing festival, and until now, I thought it would be my turn next. I expected to be a credit to my family and clan, for I was tall and strong. My grandfather and father would be able to get a good bride-price for me, I had thought. Now my aunt seemed to be saying that I might have to put all such thoughts aside.

The Gift was not merely dangerous, it seemed. It could change my life completely, perhaps in ways I did not want.

RUMORS OF A new, even harsher edict against Hebrews kept drifting through the village of Demy-en-Osiris. We heard that on an estate up the river, a midwife in another clan had obeyed this edict and smothered a newborn boy. We heard that in another village, a midwife had delivered a boy and had not smothered him. The next day, the steward's guards had beaten the midwife and torn down her hut and that of the parents. Then they had thrown the baby into the river.

As for our clan, since floodtime Aunt Shiphrah had delivered three female babies, but no boys. Puah, the midwife on the other side of the estate, had delivered one stillborn boy. So we still did not know how strictly our landlord would enforce the new edict. Steward Peneb had said nothing one way or the other, not even given a hint that he would expect a handsome bribe if we wanted him to overlook a new Hebrew boy.

So, in spite of being angry with Leah, the family was relieved that her child was a girl. But our relief did not last long. Shortly after Leah's daughter was born, *Imma* became pregnant again.

No one joked or talked about what to name the child, as they had before Aaron was born. *Imma* had dark circles under her eyes, and she dragged herself through each day. I tried to do all the extra chores, like taking the dough to the baker's and hunting for herbs in the weeds alongside the ditches.

Up on the rooftops one evening, Aunt Shiphrah joined us late, with news. "Peneb has finally spoken," she said. "Yes, he received Puah and me sitting in a carved chair outside his office, grand as Pharaoh himself. Only a little drunk."

Suddenly all the Hebrews were listening. In the hush, you could hear the Egyptians talking over in their quarter, and a dog barking outside the village.

"Of course he asked us if we were *honoring* the new decree. You want to know how Puah and I answered our steward?" Shiphrah went on, glaring around as she spoke. "Oh, we told him we were very sorry, but we couldn't promise anything. The Hebrew women are so healthy and strong that their babies are always born before the midwives arrive. And then, naturally, it is too late to smother the baby without the mother realizing, as . . ."

Letting out a moan, my mother sank to the roof-top. I put an arm around her and stared reproachfully at my aunt. My father exclaimed, "What are you thinking, brother's wife?"

"Jochabed, forgive me!" Shiphrah jumped over to our roof, her scarf flying, and seized my mother's hands. "May God curse them, the Ministry of Foreign Residents and the landlord and Steward Peneb alike! Be sure that as the Lord lives, I will see my house torn down — I will sleep outside the village with the dogs — before I let anyone harm your child."

But *Imma* pulled her hands away and clutched her knees to her chest, as if to shield the baby growing inside her. *Sabba* exclaimed, "May the Lord send quickly a second Joseph to protect us!" Aaron began to whimper.

We still did not know what would happen if my mother gave birth to a boy. But now the edict was like the blight of a *khamsin,* as the Egyptians called a dust storm. A *khamsin* began as only a faint brown haze on the southwestern horizon. But then it grew and grew, until it blotted out the sun at noon and choked the life from crops, beasts, and human beings.

CHAPTER 12

Hebrews Last

מרים

By the next baking day, the threat of the edict had faded from my mind a little. I was glad to take our bread dough to the village baker, because I always met friends and neighbors there. Of course I might also meet people I would rather not see, such as Isha-ket, the meanest woman in the village — but that could not be helped.

With a tray of unbaked loaves balanced on my head, I towed Aaron up the path through the village to the Egyptian quarter, where Satep the baker lived. He worked in his courtyard, shaded by a canopy, baking the bread in clay pots over a bed of coals.

When I arrived, the air in the courtyard was fragrant with someone's bread, and several women and girls waited their turn. Sparrows hopped and fluttered underfoot, stealing crumbs. I let Aaron loose to play with the other little children and joined my cousin Tamar in the shade of a fig tree.

"*Shalom*, Miri. Look what a messenger from Sagi's village brought over on the ferry!" Tamar showed me a silver bangle. "It is real silver! My mother said it must be worth four sheep!" It was a present from her betrothed, part of the bargain *Sabba* and Uncle Hebron had made with her future husband's family at the last sheep-shearing festival.

Admiring the gleaming circle on Tamar's wrist, I felt a strange, sad distance from my cousin and from all the grown women in our family. Would I never be betrothed, never marry, never bear children like *Imma* and Leah and Aunt Shiphrah?

On the other hand, if I never married, I would not have to leave my family. When Tamar actually married, in a year or so, she would go to live in the village of her betrothed, on the estate of another landlord, across the river. We would only see her once a year, at the shearing festival, and maybe on important occasions like a wedding or a funeral.

As Tamar chattered on about her betrothed, my mind wandered, taking in what it would mean to stay here. Gazing around the courtyard at the women chatting in twos and threes and the children chasing sparrows, I let myself feel how much I would hate to leave the village. Even the Egyptians, although we did not worship together or eat together, were decent people, and I would miss them.

My mind drifted further, and I amused myself by thinking of the people in the courtyard as a mixed herd of sheep and goats. It was easy to tell the Hebrews from the Egyptians. The Hebrew women covered their hair with headscarves, while the bare-headed Egyptian women had their hair cut in bangs over their foreheads. The Egyptian girls wore nothing but a belt of folded cloth around their hips, wide enough to carry small items, and a few trinkets such as braided bracelets and anklets, and perhaps an amulet of the household god Bes around their necks. Tamar and I and the other Hebrew girls dressed in modest tunics. The little Egyptian children wore their hair very short, except for one long sidelock. All the Hebrew children, girls and boys, had long hair.

For the most part everyone got along, although not all the Hebrew women spoke fluent Egyptian. And one of the Egyptian women, Isha-ket, made a point of being nasty to Hebrews.

An especially loud squeal drew my attention to the little children. Isha-ket's daughter, the same age as Aaron, was playing a game with him. They ran at each other with their stomachs stuck out, bounced apart, and shrieked with laughter.

I laughed too, and nudged Tamar to watch. But Isha-ket stared at the children with her hard little eyes. The small, scrawny Egyptian woman, with her beady glance and jerky movements, reminded me of a sparrow. She called to her little girl sharply, then lunged at her and yanked her arm. "You know better than to play with Eastern vermin!"

I felt a flash of anger at the look on Aaron's face. He stood in the middle of the courtyard with his stomach still stuck out, too surprised to be hurt. I wanted to scream "Heathen hag!" at Isha-ket, but I had been taught to stay out of fights. Instead I gave her a dark look as I put a hand on Aaron's curly head and drew him aside.

"Next!" shouted Satep. He was pulling a batch of baked loaves from the bed of coals, loosening them with his pointed stick from the clay baking pots, and flipping them onto a woman's tray. The last loaf, his pay for providing the pots and the fire as well as his skill, he dropped into his own basket. Satep's oldest son fed the coals with twists of straw.

All the women in the courtyard knew exactly whose turn it was, and there was never any argument about it. Now Tamar stepped forward, holding out her tray of dough.

Just then someone said, "Here comes the steward!" The hum of gossip around the courtyard died down, and we all turned to look at a group approaching along the canal path. First came two guards with spears, then the steward in his white kilt. Then a scribe, with a writing palette tucked under his arm and a reed pen behind his ear. The only person missing was the slave boy who usually carried Steward Peneb's folding stool.

That was not Peneb. I squinted in disbelief. That man following the guards was shorter than Steward Peneb. Besides, he walked with a purposeful stride, whereas Peneb swaggered, rolling from side to side.

As we stared, one of the guards called out, "Behold Steward Nakht!"

We looked uneasily at each other. "A new steward?" whispered Tamar. I was startled to realize that Peneb — our fat, boorish steward — was one of the people I might miss if I had to leave the village.

Stalking into the courtyard, the new steward paused and ran his cold gaze over the women. We bowed our heads and backed away from him. The children shrank behind their mothers and sisters, staring at the guards' spears, and I felt Aaron's fists clutching my tunic. Meanwhile, the scribe scooped a few drops of water from a jar beside the baker's fire and moistened the ink on his palette.

Not even the baker seemed to have expected the new steward. Satep, his face and chest shiny with sweat, bowed and held out his basket. "My lord steward — an honor, a very great honor! Would you do me the favor of trying these unworthy honey cakes, fresh baked at sunrise?"

Steward Peneb had *never* turned down a gift, but Steward Nakht brushed the basket aside. "Egyptians get over there," he snapped, pointing to one side of the fire. "Hebrews over there." He pointed to the other side. As we bumped into each other, murmuring apologies, in our hurry to sort ourselves out, he nodded to the scribe.

Taking the reed pen from behind his ear, the scribe counted the Egyptian women, made a note on a tablet, counted their children, and made another note. Then he did the same thing for the Hebrews. I did not like the way his pen pointed at me and Aaron as he counted. Sheep or geese were counted like this — not people.

When the scribe finished counting and gave the numbers to the steward, Nakht nodded. He turned to leave, then turned back to the baker. "Egyptians first," he rapped out to Satep. "Hebrews last."

More sweat ran down the baker's face, and he looked confused. "Yes, sir. You mean — ?"

The steward strode away without explaining, but one of the guards thumped the end of his spear on the hard ground in front of us Hebrews. "Get back. You heard what Steward Nakht said."

Most of the Egyptians seemed as stunned as we did. But Isha-ket stepped up to the bed of coals with a triumphant smile and thrust her tray at the baker. He shrugged and began dropping her dough into the baking pots. "Isha-ket was last!" protested another Egyptian woman, but it was too late.

Isha-ket strolled around the courtyard as her bread baked, talking loudly. "Yes, I have said many times, the Eastern vermin are starting to take over the Delta. Something had to be done. Praises to Nakht, our wise new steward. Egypt should be for Egyptians — you cannot deny that."

Tamar and I looked at each other. I was shocked by the fear I saw in my cousin's usually tranquil eyes, as if her expression proved to me that this evil thing was really happening.

In ordinary times, I would have been burning with anger at hateful Isha-ket. But today it seemed that she was only a speck of dust in the *khamsin* of wrath sweeping down on our clan.

CHAPTER 13

The Forbidden Baby

מרים

By the time I got back home with my baked loaves, *Imma* and my aunt had been visited by the new steward, too. My mother was in such a state, she could not stop crying. Aunt Shiphrah drew Tamar and me aside, whispering so that the young ones would not hear.

Shiphrah — my boisterous, fearless aunt — was shaking as she spoke, and she kept clasping her wrists in an odd way. First, she said, Steward Nakht told his scribe to make a special note about *Imma*, obviously pregnant. Then he had turned to Aunt Shiphrah. If she delivered any Hebrew males, he told her, he would have her hands cut off.

AND SO OUR village, our home, was transformed into a place where we never felt safe. Steward Peneb had spent much of his time dozing on his stool as he pretended to keep an eye on the estate. But Steward Nakht made a point of stalking through the village every day with his guards, enforcing all the old rules and many new ones. If a peasant caught two wild ducks in the marsh, he must hand over one to the landlord. The tenant farmers must begin work when the sun first appeared on the horizon, and not a moment later. Hebrews were not to speak to Egyptians unless spoken to.

My cousin Ephraim tested this last rule when he lost his temper and shouted at an Egyptian youth who tried to push him away from the *shaduf* in an irrigation ditch. The Egyptian ("The filthy coward!" exclaimed Ephraim) had come back to the *shaduf* with a guard, who held Ephraim's arms from behind while the other youth hit him in the face.

A few weeks later, when my mother gave birth, she would not let me try to fetch Aunt Shiphrah. I attended *Imma* by myself, praying two frantic silent prayers over and over: that the birth would be easy, and that the baby would be a girl.

The first prayer was granted; the second was not. And so our family began to attempt the impossible: hiding a baby.

At first, it went well. The other villagers did not question our story that my younger brother had been stillborn. They simply offered their condolences. Steward Nakht came the day after the birth to inspect our hut, but he did not open the duck cage in the corner near the hearth. If he had, he would have discov-

81

ered that it contained two ducks and — in a separate compartment — one baby.

At night I slept lightly, listening for the baby's slightest sounds of distress so I could comfort him before he even started to cry. When I did sleep, I was tormented by the same nightmare, over and over: Clutching Aaron, I led *Sabba, Abba,* and *Imma* through an endless swamp. We had to keep going forward, not knowing which clump of swamp grass might hold firm and which one would give way. Crocodiles waited in the brown water.

This nightmare was powerful, but not in the way that the visions of the Gift were powerful. The power in my visions came from their meaningfulness. I could feel it even when I did not understand it, as though I were watching a master craftsman shaping and cherishing his work. But the power in the nightmare was the power of a senseless urge to tear down, to smash apart, to kill.

We managed to hide the baby for one month, then two — almost three. *Sabba* wove a larger duck cage, although we still had only two ducks. We did not talk about the baby if we could help it, or even name him, as if that would bring bad luck.

There were narrow escapes. Once Aaron announced to his cousin Rachel, as an Egyptian guard walked by, "I am a big brother now." Another time, as *Imma* was in the hut feeding the baby, a neighbor came to the door to borrow oil. Just then the baby belched loudly, and the neighbor looked startled. I had to pretend that *Imma* had indigestion.

Then one morning when I was down at the canal, washing the family laundry, a shadow fell across my arms. I looked over my shoulder to see Isha-ket on the bank, staring down at me — or rather, at the linen I was washing. My heart seemed to stop beating. Surely no one could make out a baby's swaddling cloths among the loincloths and shifts?

I watched from the corner of my eye as Isha-ket joined the other Egyptian women at the water's edge. I caught a few words of what she was saying while she beat her clothes on the rocks: " . . . have my eye on them . . . would not put it past those Eastern vermin . . ."

I was reluctant to upset *Imma*, but I felt I had to tell her. That evening, *Sabba* called a family conference. We all knew that a terrible decision must be made. Aunt Shiphrah and Uncle Hebron joined my mother and father and grandfather in our hut, hot and stuffy as it was, so that even friendly ears on the rooftops could not hear us. Aaron and I sat on the sleeping platform, wide awake. Lamplight flickered over the circle of adults on the floor. *Imma* fed the baby. No one spoke, and the baby's sucking sounded alarmingly loud.

Finally *Sabba* lifted his hands and began to pray. "Lord God, we have kept your child safe as long as we could. If it is your will for him to live, reveal to us what to do, I beg you."

"We beg you, Lord," the rest of us murmured.

Then my grandfather beckoned to me. I knew at once what he intended, and I trembled. I looked at the other adults, expecting them to protest, but their desperate faces simply looked back at me.

Once again *Sabba* placed his hands on my head and began to pray over me, as he had the night they discussed the gold duck pendant. I had thought my family was frightened then — now I knew what real terror was. But as my grandfather's mellow voice filled the hut, a calmness came over me. I began to feel strong, with a strength beyond myself. My baby brother's life — the lives of all of us — depended on me using the Gift, or perhaps the Gift using me. So be it.

THAT NIGHT I dreamed that the earth was flooded, as in the story of our ancestor Noah. An ark floated on the water. At first I thought it *was* Noah's ark.

But then the dream shifted, and I realized that I was looking at something much smaller than an ark. It was a basket, about the size of the duck cage we had been hiding my baby brother in. It floated among the reeds at the edge of the river.

The basket was ordinary, a tight weave daubed with pitch for waterproofing. But there was a glow around it. And from inside came a baby's indignant wail.

CHAPTER 14

A Gift from a God

The outing on the river had been Nebet's idea. She
hoped it would calm Princess Bint-Anath to get
out of the palace and spend the afternoon swimming.
Besides, if the princess were away from the palace, she
could not be called to the King's quarters to play
sennet with him. And then he could not notice that
she was *not* wearing her gold duck pendant, as she
had promised him she would the next time they met
together.

The princess herself, although she had treated the
missing pendant like a joke at first, seemed anxious
now. The trouble was, when the princess was worried,
she did not react like a sensible person — like Nebet,
for instance. Nebet, when worried, immediately began to plan how to solve the problem.

But Princess Bint-Anath put on a hard smile,

laughed a high, brittle laugh, and began to do one reckless thing after another. The other day she had repeated some embarrassing gossip — not exactly true, but not exactly false — about her mother to one of the lesser wives. Of course the rumor, including its source, had gotten back to Queen Ystnefert. She was furious. Yesterday the Queen had summoned Nebet and made a suggestion: perhaps Nebet would like to join her coterie.

Nebet had a justly high opinion of her own worth as a lady-in-waiting, but she was not fooled by the Queen's compliments. Ystnefert knew how much Princess Bint-Anath counted on Nebet, and she wanted to punish her daughter by taking away her head lady-in-waiting. Kneeling before the Queen's ivory footstool, Nebet had a traitorous thought: Why not accept the offer?

In the beginning, Nebet had chosen to attend Princess Bint-Anath simply because she was Pharaoh's favorite daughter. The chief lady-in-waiting of such a princess could expect to share in the power and privileges of that favor. Then, as the years went by, Nebet took increasing pride in her skill at handling the temperamental princess, managing her household, and using her own position to gather influence.

And finally. . . . Sensible as she was, Nebet had come to feel a deep affection for the unhappy princess. She was difficult, she was unreasonable, she was often maddening — but she was also *so* lovely, *so* graceful, and she could charm even Nebet with her playfulness. Besides, there was a wistful quality about her that seemed to plead, "Be kind, for I am denied my heart's desire." Bint-Anath was like the daughter Nebet had never had.

So Nebet had politely declined to change posts, and the Queen had let it go for the moment. But if the Queen decided to make an issue of it, she could have any lady-in-waiting she liked for herself.

NOW, AS Princess Bint-Anath's barge, with the usual number of her attendants, backed away from the palace dock, Nebet stared gloomily up at the statue of the King and his dearest daughter. While Bint-Anath remained Pharaoh's favorite, no one would disrespect her or those who served her. But if she ever fell out of favor, everyone would know it. To begin with, her statue would be carefully and thoroughly chipped away from the knee of His Majesty's statue. Nebet shuddered at the prospect.

The crew raised the sail, and the barge turned upriver. Sitting back under the striped awning, Nebet breathed a little easier. It would do *her* good to be out of the palace, too. Overhead the sail swelled in the wind from the north, and the barge rocked gently over the wavelets. It was the beginning of *shemu*, the harvest season, the most beautiful time of year.

Nebet had instructed the captain to sail to a quiet inlet bordered by a papyrus marsh. It was a sheltered, pleasant place for a swim and refreshments. The reeds were full grown at this season, and birds sang as they perched on the tufts and ate the seeds. Wild ducks and geese paddled through the stands of papyrus.

As soon as the barge was anchored, Bint-Anath let her robe fall to the deck and dove off the side. Nebet and the other ladies joined her in the water. The princess swam around the inlet, then finally turned over to float on her back. She gave a deep sigh and smiled at her head lady-in-waiting.

"Nebet," murmured the princess, "you always know what is best for me. You will never leave me, will you?"

Nebet's heart skipped a beat. Had the princess somehow heard about the Queen's offer? "Never, Your Highness."

The princess righted herself and embraced her, pressing her cheek against Nebet's. Then she pulled away and exclaimed in a light tone, "Oh, look at the ducks, coming around the end of the barge. Do you not love ducks, Nebet? Are they not dear, the way they stick their tails up when they dabble?"

Then, as Princess Bint-Anath pushed her damp hair back from her face, something seemed to catch her eye. Her whole body tensed, and her gaze fixed on an object bobbing among the ducks. "What is *that!*" she whispered.

"That" was a dark oval about the size of a goose. Nebet had seen it already without paying much attention; she had thought it was some kind of waterfowl, because it seemed to be swimming with the ducks. But it was not a bird at all. It was a reed box or basket, floating along in the wake of the ducks.

A guard on the end of the barge saw the basket, too. Lifting his eyebrows in idle curiosity, he leaned over to jab it with his spear. But he stopped with his arm raised as the basket let out a piercing wail.

Then Princess Bint-Anath's voice rang out in a fully royal tone, although she was dripping water and wearing nothing, not even her wig. "Halt, guard! Nebet, quickly — bring me that basket."

The lady-in-waiting swam over to the barge and swam back to the princess, pushing the basket. There was nothing else to do, although she already knew what was inside. Only a baby squalled like that. And the weave of the pitch-caulked basket was clearly Hebrew. Nebet remembered the new decree from the Ministry of Foreign Residents, and she thought, Surely this is the result.

The princess pried eagerly at the basket, but Nebet had to help her open it. The lid was fastened down with several catches and smeared with pitch. Finally, as all the women crowded around to see, the basket opened.

Inside was indeed a baby, about three months old. He (Nebet was sure it was a boy) was wrapped in swaddling bands and cradled in lambswool. His face, screwed up to wail again, was as red as henna.

"Poor little baby!" exclaimed Princess Bint-Anath. "Where did you come from?"

Nebet was silent, but she glanced at the other women to see if any of them had recognized the weave of the basket. Perhaps she was the only one.

With a dreamy expression on her lovely face, Bint-

Anath lifted the baby from his nest. Immediately he stopped crying. "Ah-ah," cooed the princess. The baby's face broke into a toothless smile. "Ah-ah," he answered.

Nebet was in the habit of weighing every new situation to figure out how to manage it. But at this moment she stood like a statue, too astonished to move or even think. Then the gleam of gold caught her eye. Something shiny was swinging from a cord around the baby's neck, hanging down his back. Making a wordless sound, Nebet pointed.

Princess Bint-Anath turned the baby around to see what Nebet was gaping at. Then her eyes widened, and she drew a deep breath.

"Praise to Osiris!" The princess held the baby up and turned him this way and that, so that all the women could see the gold flashing in the sun. "The baby wears *my pendant,* the same one I lost in the Nile! Can anyone doubt that it is a sign?" She sobbed, an unashamed sob of joy. "The god has sent me a child on the river! Behold — Mose!"

The other women hastened to exclaim over the baby. "A miracle!" "Such a handsome, healthy child!" "Oh, praise to Osiris for his goodness to Your Highness!"

Only Nebet was stunned into silence. Mose — "son." For an instant she wondered if Princess Bint-Anath could somehow have arranged for this to happen. But she was not an arranger, like Nebet. Perhaps it really was a gift from Osiris — except why would he choose a *Hebrew* baby?

The princess, calmer again, was cuddling the baby. "I wonder where I can find a dependable wet nurse for my Mose?"

That was something Nebet could arrange, and she finally found her voice. Because she made it her business to keep track of all the babies in the palace and keep them out of the princess's sight, she knew of several women who had just had babies and could feed another one. "There is your own hairdresser, Your Highness. Or what about the seventeenth sister of Your Highness's personal maid? Or — "

Just when Nebet thought she could never be any more surprised than she was at that moment, there was a shout from the nearest stand of papyrus. "I know a nurse!" They all turned to see a girl splashing her way out of the reeds.

A few yards from the Egyptian women, the girl stopped, glancing from the guards on the barge to the princess and her ladies. She looked terrified by her own boldness, but she bowed as low as she could in the water.

"O Pharaoh's daughter, m-may you live and prosper. I — I know a clean, reliable woman who — Because she just lost her own child, she would nurse that baby so well for you! She would care for him as if — as if he were her own."

For the second time in one afternoon, Nebet was dumbfounded. This girl who had just burst out of the reeds like a startled heron — was she not the same Hebrew girl who had wandered into the garden at the villa, when they were waiting for the barge to be repaired? Nebet was sure of it. She was well-favored, with an intelligent look.

Too intelligent, thought Nebet suspiciously. Had the girl somehow arranged — No, impossible. She could not have known that Princess Bint-Anath would come here to swim today.

Nebet wondered if the princess recognized the girl, too. Bint-Anath seemed to swallow a smile. "As if he were her own," she repeated. "How ideal. Of course, Mose is *mine*. For the god has sent him to me on the river."

"Just as you say, Pharaoh's daughter," answered the girl. Her voice trembled as she looked at the baby in Princess Bint-Anath's arms. "God has sent him to you."

CHAPTER 15

To the Palace

מרים

When I arrived at our hut, *Sabba* was outside, rocking back and forth and chanting prayers, and Aaron was doing his best to imitate him. From inside came the mingled wailing of *Imma* and Aunt Shiphrah. But then I gasped out my news, and my grandfather and brother both jumped up, *Sabba* almost as spry as Aaron. The three of us burst into the hut, where my mother and aunt huddled together on the sleeping platform. Their hair was wild and smeared with ashes, as if for mourning.

As soon as they could take in what I was saying, my mother and aunt scrambled to their feet, too. With only a few moments' work, and in spite of us all exclaiming at once and hugging each other and getting in each other's way, *Imma* turned into the "clean, reliable woman" I had promised. She had on her festival tunic, her face was washed, and her hair was combed and covered with a neat scarf. She and I hurried down the canal path to the river.

On the deck of the barge, after *Imma* and I prostrated ourselves before Princess Bint-Anath, I watched the princess and her chief lady-in-waiting look over my mother. I was seized with worry. *I* knew *Imma* could take better care of our baby than anyone else in the world, but how could they know that?

I seemed to see my mother through the eyes of these women, especially the lady-in-waiting, whom the princess called Nebet. I looked at my mother's humble, sincere face, and listened to her begging for the job in her broken Egyptian. How did she compare with all the palace-trained Egyptian servants they might hire? Still, if the princess believed that the baby was sent to her on the river, perhaps she would believe this nurse was also sent.

Princess Bint-Anath glanced at Nebet, raising her eyebrows. Nebet gave a barely visible nod. I let out a long breath. "You will do," said the princess to my mother. "Lady Nebet will arrange for you to be brought to the palace, and paid, and so on."

My mother bowed, stammering thanks, but I saw her body stiffen. With a shock, I realized what the result of this miracle would be. My baby brother was saved — but at the price of being adopted by a stranger, not even a Hebrew stranger. And my timid mother would have to leave us and go live among heathens in the palace.

With a further shock, I realized that the princess

was now gazing straight at *me*. "And you, bold girl — you may come to the palace, too. You can make yourself useful by translating for the wet nurse." Lady Nebet looked concerned and murmured something to the princess, but Princess Bint-Anath only laughed. "How you worry, Nebet! It gives *me* no pause. Besides — the girl amuses me."

Just like that. On the whim of Pharaoh's daughter, the course of my life was changed.

Quickly Lady Nebet instructed a few of the guards. They were to escort me and my mother, with the baby, back to our village to gather our belongings. "If any of the landlord's men try to interfere," I heard her say, "get their names."

We must have been the strangest procession that ever marched through Demy-en-Osiris: a Hebrew woman, baby, and girl escorted by royal guards. I saw Isha-ket standing in the door of her hut with her mouth open. Then she darted off, dragging her little girl, and I was sure she was going to tell Steward Nakht.

The rest of the neighbors seemed to be torn between curiosity and fear. They kept out of sight of the guards, but I glimpsed faces peering out of doorways and around corners. Steward Nakht himself stalked purposefully up to our hut, but at the sight of the royal guards, he came to a dead halt. I think he would have sneaked quietly away if the captain of the princess's guards had not ordered him to stop.

I did not hear what the guards asked Steward Nakht, because I was scrambling around the hut, getting together a bundle of belongings. Our few clothes, a comb, *Imma's* hand loom. . . . Stepping outside, I found my aunt and cousins waiting, and my mother sobbing as she said good-bye to each one. Of course all the able-bodied men, including my father and Uncle Hebron and Cousin Ephraim, were still in the fields. There was no time to wait until they came home, or to walk out to the fields and say good-bye to them.

I felt a stab of panic, as if the hard-packed dirt were sliding out from under my feet. I turned and stared at the mud-brick hut where I had lived for all of my eleven years. My gaze fell on the ladder to the roof, leaning against the side wall, and on the woven mat tied back from the doorway. There was the hateful grindstone on one side of the doorway, and a bundle of *Sabba's* dried reeds on the other. This scene — my home — suddenly seemed no more solid than a reflection in the canal.

Aunt Shiphrah stepped forward and gave me a fierce hug, as if to remind me how solid she was. "Look after your *Imma* and your baby brother, Miri."

Tamar hugged me, too, but she seemed to look at me as if *I* were a reflection, dissolving into ripples. "My cousin! My dearest friend! At least promise you will come back for my wedding," she whispered.

Tamar's wedding, not until the next shearing festival! At the thought of staying away that long, I burst into tears. "I promise!" Quickly I hugged all the little cousins in turn, hardly noticing which was which.

Then Aaron fell into my arms. "Take me, Miwi!"

By this time, everyone was sobbing except my

grandfather. "Hush," he said sternly to Aaron. "They must go, and we must stay."

Imma and I knelt for *Sabba's* blessing, and he rested his knobby hands on our heads. "The Lord go with you, and keep you. Praise the Lord God, who has answered our prayers. May this child Miriam and her Gift always serve her people and their God."

As he finished the last word, the captain of the princess's guard knocked his spear butt on the ground. "Pharaoh's daughter is not to be kept waiting."

With our bundle balanced on my head and the baby in a corner of my mother's shawl, we followed the guards back down the canal path. It struck me that this was the third time I had walked to the river this afternoon. The first time, I had helped *Imma* carry my baby brother in his little ark, fearing that we would be launching him to his death. The second time, I had brought my mother to the princess, who was taking our baby. And this time, I was leaving the village where I had been born. I was going to live in the palace of King Rameses.

The first two times I walked to the river, I had not even thought of looking back. But now, outside the Egyptian quarter of the village, I glanced over my shoulder. Against the back wall of the baker's house stood a whole crowd, squinting into the late-afternoon sun. All the women and children in the village must be there, I thought. Nothing like this had ever happened in Demy-en-Osiris before.

At the river, guards helped us climb up into the

princess's barge. Princess Bint-Anath rose from her seat under the awning, her face alight as she held out her arms. "Mose," she cooed, cuddling my baby brother. "My dear little Mose."

"What did the princess say?" whispered *Imma* as the guards showed us to our place at the aft end of the barge, near the pilot.

"She calls him by the name she gave him, 'Mose,'" I whispered back.

My mother winced. "He is not an Egyptian baby, to be given an Egyptian name! *I* name him Moshe."

I did not remind her that our baby was alive only because he had been taken in as an Egyptian baby. I turned my face away from the sun, now low over the western bank. The guards chatted among themselves and called out to soldiers on other boats, but my mother and I fell silent.

I had paddled our boat down this stretch of the river many times, on my way to market with *Sabba*, but the route looked different now that my destination was the palace. At last the towers of the palace gates loomed downriver. The setting sun lit up the statue of the King above the docks. Swinging the barge around, the crew pulled it up to a mooring. The great gilded gates of the palace were flung open for Princess Bint-Anath, and *Imma* and I followed her and her women up the steps from the dock. We three Hebrews of the clan of Levi were swallowed up by this unknown world.

CHAPTER 16

Lost in the Palace

מרים

From the palace entrance, Princess Bint-Anath and her women went in one direction, their way lit by servants with torches. As for *Imma* and Moshe and me, a guard led us through the palace grounds. The guard had no trouble finding his way by starlight, but we seemed to be stumbling endlessly down dark alleys and alongside huge buildings and around fences. At last we reached the gate of an enclosure with several low buildings. "The women servants' quarters," the guard told me. He knocked on the gate with his spear butt. "Gatekeeper!"

The gatekeeper seemed annoyed to have to put down his jar of beer, but he let us into the courtyard and went off to find the servants' housekeeper. As we stood waiting, the music of drums and flutes, as well as bursts of laughter, came from somewhere outside the servants' quarters. After a time the gatekeeper returned and sat down by the gate again. Moshe began to squirm and whimper.

"Why does the housekeeper not come?" whispered my mother. "Should we present ourselves to her?"

Reluctantly, I questioned the gatekeeper in Egyptian. He only frowned and said, "Wait, peasants."

A few minutes later a woman appeared, carrying a lamp and followed by a yawning girl with mats on her shoulder. The housekeeper's well-fed face had a pleasant expression, but her glance went to our striped tunics, as if wondering what to do with the Hebrews. "I suppose there is more room for you in this first hall," she decided, pointing to a doorway off the courtyard.

Inside the hall, the housekeeper held the lamp while the slave unrolled our sleeping mats, and I gazed around. The hall seemed enormous, more like a granary than a sleeping space. I wondered why no one else was already asleep in here. There were mats enough laid out along the length of the sleeping platform, and it was well after dark.

Then the housekeeper and her slave were gone. I was hungry and thirsty, but I was also bone-tired. I heard *Imma's* weary sigh as she lay down, and the sound of the baby's contented sucking. I lay down, too, snuggling up to my mother and baby brother. The three of us made a comforting cluster in that big empty space.

Later, I half-woke at footsteps and voices in the hall. It was still dark, and I managed to go back to sleep until someone stumbled over my legs, cursing.

"Tail of Taweret!" exclaimed a shrill voice. "Who is in my space?"

"Hold your noise, Hunro!" called another female voice, from the other side of the hall. Other girls or women joined in. "For the love of Bes, be quiet!" "Who let her drink so much wine?"

Beside me my mother asked, "Miri? Who are they? What do they want?" The baby began to wail.

To get some peace, *Imma* and I finally dragged our mats out into the courtyard. She spread her shawl over the three of us, and she and Moshe went back to sleep, as I could tell by their slow, even breathing. But I looked up at the stars and wondered how we could bear to dwell for months — no, *years*, before Moshe could be weaned — in this huge, strange place where no one cared for us.

IN THE MORNING, we were awakened by the servants gathering in the courtyard for breakfast. I watched the young women come out of the first sleeping hall, braiding each other's hair and fastening their belts. Like the Egyptian girls in our village, they wore only belts and jewelry. But while the peasant girls of Demy-en-Osiris seemed merely unclothed, these palace girls looked deliberately naked. They stared at us, giggling and making comments, and *Imma* stared back. "The Lord keep us from unclean ways," she muttered.

It was my mother's place to take bread before I did, and to say where we should eat. But *Imma* had a helpless, lost look, and I was afraid we would go hungry if I waited for her. Across the courtyard I spotted a group of modestly dressed women. "Let us join those other nurses and babies," I suggested. I wanted to get away from the palace girls, too. They would not understand my mother's Hebrew words, but her looks said "harlots" plainly enough. And some of them seemed tough enough to pull hair or scratch if they got angry.

We took bread from the baskets and sat on a bench near the group of women with little ones. One of the nurses, a woman with a girl about a year old, cooed at our baby and tried to strike up a conversation with *Imma*. With me translating, they exchanged a few remarks.

The woman's name was Kawit, and she was caring for the little daughter of one of the King's concubines, Sitamun. Kawit urged *Imma* to help herself to beer ("so good for the milk") from a jug especially for the wet nurses. But my mother had never drunk beer in her life, and she would not drink it now, even to be polite. We drank from the tall water jugs beside the courtyard gate.

All this time, Kawit had been throwing curious glances at Moshe in my mother's arms. Finally she leaned forward and whispered, "Is it true what they say, that Osiris sent that child to her highness on the river?"

I was so surprised that this story had already gotten around the palace, I did not try to answer, but repeated the question in Hebrew for my mother. "What a false, heathen story!" she exclaimed, hugging the baby to her. "My Moshe has nothing to do with Egyptian gods."

What was the matter with *Imma*? She ought to see that this "false" story was Moshe's best protection. I gave Kawit an apologetic shrug. "My mother does not like to speak of this," I explained. "She — she is afraid it is too great a responsibility, to care for such a blessed baby."

I was so busy translating for my mother and Kawit that it took me a long time to eat. I was swallowing the last bite and watching the palace girls go out the gate when the housekeeper came up to us. "You, girl — you had better go along with the other dancing girls, or you will be late, and the music master will be angry."

When I began to protest, she interrupted me kindly but firmly. "What? Of course you are expected to go. You have to make yourself useful in the palace, you know."

Imma was suspicious of my translation. "How can you do your share of hauling water and grinding grain," my mother asked, "if you are at 'music practice' — whatever that might be?" But the housekeeper repeated herself, looking impatient, and I thought I had better do what she said. "Be careful!" called *Imma* as I ran out of the gate.

Outside the servants' quarters, I paused uncertainly. The dancing girls were already out of sight. Ahead of me, mounted on broad steps, was a pavilion, its pillars decorated with picture-writing and figures of people, animals, and animal-headed gods. Servants were at work, unwinding wilted garlands from the pillars, carrying chairs and tables down the steps, and picking up duck bones. There must have been a feast here last night — was that where the dancing girls had stayed out so late?

But the dancing girls were not in the pavilion now, and I had to find them. I started for a row of open-sided sheds beyond the pavilion. They were weavers' sheds, like the one where my sister Leah worked at the villa, and the weavers were now gathering, chatting as they took their places at the looms. I stepped up to the nearest woman, arranging her spindles of thread, and asked if she had seen a group of dancing girls go by.

She looked me up and down with a quizzical smile. Then she said, "Toward the stables," with a jerk of her head. As I left in the direction she had pointed out, I half-heard a remark the weaver made to her neighbor, with a snicker. Something about a little peasant girl and those brazen dancers.

But I did not stop to wonder who was being insulted, or how. I hurried toward a fenced field, where glossy-coated horses whinnied and cavorted. A statue of King Rameses smiled down on the grooms exercising his steeds. And there were the dancing girls, leaning on the stable-yard fence.

Horses, more of them than I could count at a glance! Sir Satepihu owned *one* horse, which he grandly drove in his chariot in processions. These animals were a great luxury, for they had no real use except in war.

I glanced at the other girls, wanting to share my feeling about seeing all these sleek, powerful horses at once. But the dancing girls were interested in the grooms, not the horses. The men called out suggestive remarks, and the girls laughed and tossed their heads. I blushed, although the grooms were not flirting with me.

The girls strolled off, and I followed them between two statues of King Rameses and through an arcade of columns carved and painted to look like bundles of papyrus. At the end of the arcade, a craftsman balanced on a ladder with a paint pot hanging from his neck. He was painting the feathery tips of the papyrus with gilt paint. I wanted to stop and watch him work, but the other girls were moving on.

Then something on the floor caught my eye, and I looked down and gasped. I was *walking* on the most beautiful painting I had ever seen! It showed, among the reeds and pools of a marsh, a nobleman aiming his arrow at wild geese. His striped hunting cat leaped out of the reeds onto a duck, and his wife gathered a basket of lotus blossoms.

Just in time I noticed that the other girls were disappearing around a corner, and I hurried to catch up with them again. Past another statue of King Rameses, there was an entrance to a spacious courtyard. Musicians were busy carrying instruments out of a storage room. I had never seen so many instruments together, even on feast days: flutes, double flutes, tambourines, lyres, lutes, bronze cymbals, drums.

The girls bowed respectfully to one of the musicians, and I gathered that he was the music master. I wondered if I ought to tell him who I was, but he rapped out, "Places, dancers!" He began clapping the time, and the musicians struck up a tune. I lined up with the other girls and tried to do what they did.

I was used to dancing with the other Hebrew girls and women on feast days, and I loved the feeling of being lifted up and carried along by the music with the other dancers. But these were different rhythms and steps, and I had to pay close attention in order to keep up.

Then the music master had us work on acrobatic routines. I was astonished at how easily the other girls slid into splits and arched their backs into hoops. I tried to imitate them, but I fell on the floor with painful thumps. And high kicks I could not do at all in my calf-length tunic.

Putting his hands up, the music master stopped the practice. "You!" Yes, he was glaring at me. "The girl in the striped grain sack. Take it off, for Hathor's sake!"

I stood there with my gaze on the ground. One of the girls whispered, "She is in for a beating." The music master's scowl deepened, and I was afraid he would come over and strike me. But I could *not* take off my tunic in front of strangers, not even if they threw me into a dungeon like my ancestor Joseph.

Then I had an idea: I tucked my tunic between my legs and into my sash. I did that sometimes at home, cutting papyrus reeds in the marsh. It seemed like a sensible compromise to me — my legs would be free, but my dress would not be too immodest.

But the music master burst out laughing, and the musicians and girls joined in. "Now *that* is an alluring costume," said the music master. "What was Lady Nebet thinking of?" he added, as if to himself. "I will certainly take it up with her later. Continue!" he commanded the musicians.

The laughter died down, and the drum and flutes started up again. My face felt as red as if I had been bending over a hearth.

At the end of that long morning, I hurried off by myself, to avoid walking back with the dancing girls. I got lost on my way back to the servants' quarters, but I hated to ask directions from any of the people rushing busily past me. At one point I came upon the bakery, and watched a row of women working at grindstones. I almost envied them their place in the palace world.

Beyond the bakery stretched a vegetable garden as large as a wheat field. Gardeners were pouring water into the irrigation channels and spreading manure on the neat square plots. Manure from all those horses, no doubt! My mind boggled at the luxury of such an enormous vegetable garden, all fed by horse manure. No wonder the lettuces were as large as shrubs.

As I wandered on, it seemed that around every corner there was another image of King Rameses. He was standing or sitting; he wore his double crown, or a curled wig; he was life-size, or as tall as the pillars of the arcades. Even outside the women servants' gate, as I noticed when I finally found it, there was a small clay statue of the King. I wanted to get away from him, but he was everywhere.

CHAPTER 17

Homesick

מרים

That afternoon, after the midday rest, the servants' housekeeper told me to bathe Moshe and wrap him in fresh linen and take him to Princess Bint-Anath. "I will take him," protested *Imma* when I told her.

I asked the housekeeper, but she shook her head. "Lady Nebet said the Hebrew *girl* was to bring the baby. It is wise to do exactly as Lady Nebet directs."

So holding my fresh, clean baby brother against my shoulder, I set out for the princess's garden, on the other side of the palace grounds. I got lost again, but now that I had a purpose, I did not mind asking the way. Besides, the people I met were charmed by Moshe. As they were talking to me, they would coo to him and coax him to smile.

As I stood outside the gate of the walled garden, I

breathed in a drift of flower scent. Over the humming of bees sounded the notes of a plucked lute. After glancing toward Lady Nebet for approval, the guard let me in the gate, and I stepped into a place like *Sabba's* descriptions of the Garden of Eden.

Blooming acacia trees framed the entrance with yellow clouds like duckling fluff. Farther into the garden, a lady stood under a date palm, calling up to a monkey. "Look, Moshe," I whispered. "The monkey is picking dates for her!"

A sharp clap from Lady Nebet drew my attention to a pool beyond the date tree. I had been told to bring the baby to the princess, I remembered, not to take my time gawking at her garden.

Behind Lady Nebet, Princess Bint-Anath sat at the edge of the pool, shaded by silvery-leaved olive trees. Her feet dangled in the water, and reflected light shimmered over her finely chiseled features. At the sight of me with Moshe, she scrambled to her feet — a little undignified for a princess. I knelt before her and watched her elegant face go soft with joy as she took the baby in her arms.

Lady Nebet motioned me to retreat behind the olive trees, then called a slave to pour a bowl of goat's milk from a jar kept in the pool. Dipping her slim, beringed fingers into the milk, Princess Bint-Anath let the baby suck them. I watched in fascination. It was as if the princess were dreaming a beautiful dream of being a mother, without any of the work. Of course they would not want *Imma* to bring the baby to the garden. Moshe's real mother would not fit into this scene at all.

No one told me to do anything, so I stayed out of the way and watched, wide-eyed. The ladies tossed bright-colored balls back and forth in the shade of the fruit trees, or played board games under a jasmine arbor, or lounged in a little boat on the pool, gossiping. I kept expecting one of them to take out a spindle or a hand loom, or work on a basket, or at least string beads. But all afternoon, as I watched, Princess Bint-Anath's ladies did nothing useful. They did not even make music, for the servants played the lute and sang for them. I began to feel light-headed, as if I were drifting down a river made of melody and perfume.

When the shadows were long, Lady Nebet beckoned me back to the poolside to take the baby from Princess Bint-Anath. "Until tomorrow, my duckling," murmured the princess, kissing him on his nose.

I was glad my brother had been so content with the princess. But at the same time, I thought he should have noticed the difference between her and *Imma*. Once outside the garden, I whispered in his ear, "Do not forget: you are a Hebrew of the clan of Levi, descendant of Abraham and Joseph."

BY EVENING I was weary. I had done no real work myself that day, but I was tired of being around strangers, and of hearing nothing but Egyptian. It was like having to live in the market at Pi-Rameses instead of visiting and then going home.

I longed for a private place to eat supper with my

mother, but there was nowhere except the courtyard, shared by all the servants.

A woman lit the lamps on stands around the courtyard while others carried in baskets of bread, platters of fish, and jugs of beer. *Imma* and I sat on one end of a bench, and she said a blessing over our food, and we both chanted an evening hymn. But our two voices sounded thin and uncertain, and the other servants stared at us.

After supper, the dancing girls left for their evening work, the other servants went off to their sleeping halls, and we spread our mats in the courtyard again. I buried my face in my mother's shoulder, taking comfort from the familiar smell of wool and herbs. "My throat hurts," I whispered, "and my chest aches. Am I falling ill with floodtime fever?"

"No," said *Imma*. To my relief, her voice sounded firm and reasuring for the first time that day. "You are homesick," she went on. "I felt the same way when I was first married and came to our village." With a catch in her voice, she added, "I thought I would never feel homesick, ever again."

We huddled together, with Moshe between us. I thought of our ancestor Joseph, sold into slavery in Egypt and then thrown into a dungeon. It must have been bitter to be a slave, and more bitter still to be shut up in a dark place. But I thought the hardest part for Joseph must have been the moment he was pulled out of the pit. He would have expected to see his brothers' faces, ashamed and perhaps still angry with him, at the other end of the rope. Instead, he had

111

looked into the uncaring faces of strangers. They were hauling him up not to rescue him, but to carry him away from his father's tent forever.

But I was not a slave, I reminded myself. I was not in a dungeon, and at least I had my mother and baby brother with me. Still, I longed to be on the rooftop of our hut with the clan all around.

I thought of the Gift by which I had helped to save our Moshe. *Sabba* had said God meant me to use the Gift for our people. How strange, then, that the workings of the Gift had *separated* me from the clan.

The same thing had happened with Joseph, I remembered with a sinking feeling. He came to Egypt when he was seventeen, and he did not see his family again for many years. How did he bear it? How could *I* bear it?

CHAPTER 18

Hebrews in the Palace

Three Hebrews! And one of them a baby boy! Why, *why*, Nebet asked herself, had she not at least prevented the princess from hiring the Hebrew wet nurse? Instead, she had stood there on the barge, nodding like a half-wit.

Well, now Nebet would just have to wait patiently for the princess to fall out of love with her "Mose," and perhaps fall in love with a suitable Egyptian child that Nebet would present. After all, not so long ago Bint-Anath had sworn that Imiu, a hairdresser she had lured away from another princess, would be her hairdresser for life. Imiu had a divine gift for arranging royal hair, Bint-Anath insisted, ignoring Nebet's warning that Imiu had a loose tongue and would spread the princess's secrets all over the palace. Bint-Anath made a special offering to Hathor for Imiu's protection, she encouraged Imiu to eat from her dish, and she even talked of giving Imiu a small plot of land.

Nebet had bided her time and made preparations. On a nobleman's estate she had found a talented, ambitious hairdresser, a young woman named Senen, who readily came to an understanding with Princess Bint-Anath's head lady-in-waiting. When Bint-Anath had finally decided that Imiu was untrustworthy and ungrateful, she had allowed Nebet to replace her with the reliable Senen.

Now Nebet must calmly plan how to get the Hebrews out of Pi-Rameses. This would not be easy or quick, for it must be done quietly, and the princess must believe it was her own decision. Meanwhile, every time Nebet remembered that those Hebrews were right here in the King's house (may he live and prosper), under the protection of Princess Bint-Anath, she went cold all over. If the High Priest of Amon-Re found out, he would surely use the information against the King. Then Princess Bint-Anath would be out of favor with her father for good.

Two days after the Hebrews arrived at the palace, the royal music master stopped Nebet outside the entrance to the Grand Reception Hall. "Lady Nebet, if I might have the favor of a word with you — " His bow was stiff, his tone angrily polite. "That Eastern peasant girl you sent to dance practice is hopeless. No, I do not mean clumsy. She is graceful enough, but what does that matter if she insists on wearing a thick wool tunic? I do not know how she expects to catch the eye of a lord, covered with that blanket."

Nebet clucked sympathetically and promised to speak to the girl. She was surprised, for she had thought the Hebrew girl was intelligent enough to learn how to swim with the current, so to speak. Why would she balk at dancing without her tunic? But Nebet was not displeased. If the girl was difficult, it would be easier to convince the princess to send her away.

In the meantime, Nebet needed to prevent word from spreading about the Hebrews that the princess had brought home. Nebet was not really worried about the princess's servants or ladies. They were all thrilled that they had witnessed a miracle with her highness, so they were not thinking of the baby as a Hebrew. And besides, very likely they did not think the princess had to be careful about angering the High Priest. No, Nebet was more concerned about the steward of the estate the Hebrews had come from. According to what the captain of the princess's guards had told her, Steward Nakht was as zealous against Hebrews as the High Priest of Amon-Re could wish.

Only a few days after the princess found the baby, Nebet took a boat up the river to Satepihu's villa. She sent her guard into the village of Demy-en-Osiris to find out what he could about the Hebrew girl and woman. She herself paid a call on Satepihu's wife. Over refreshments in the garden, Nebet suggested that Princess Bint-Anath might decide to invite Satepihu and his family to the anniversary celebration of the King's coronation. Then she tactfully made clear what the price was: the steward must be dismissed.

"Oh! But Sir Satepihu says — but he is pleased with Steward Nakht," the lady of the villa said doubtfully. "Nakht is making the lazy tenant farmers work much harder than Steward Peneb did. And he will not take bribes."

Exactly, you foolish woman, thought Nebet. She murmured into her cool drink, "Her highness would regret it so deeply if you could not, after all, sit beside her at the celebration, but . . ."

On the boat, returning to the palace, the guard informed Nebet that the Hebrew woman and girl were mother and daughter, decent people. "The villagers, Hebrew and Egyptian alike, speak well of Kohath's family."

This was reassuring news. If the princess must have Hebrews in the palace for a time, it was well that they were Hebrews of good reputation.

Shortly after her visit to Satepihu's villa, Nebet heard that the landlord's wife had managed to get rid of Nakht. This was only what Nebet had expected — but the *way* she received the news startled her.

It was on an afternoon in Princess Bint-Anath's garden. The other ladies were amusing themselves as usual, and the princess strolled along the shaded paths with Mose in her arms. Nebet stood at one end of the pool, discussing with a sculptor and a stonemason the placement of a new shrine to Osiris. The princess had ordered it built to show her gratitude to the god for sending her a son.

"My lady." The Hebrew girl Mery, or whatever her name was, bowed as the lady-in-waiting turned from the craftsmen. "On behalf of my grandfather, Kohath the Storyteller, head of the clan of Levi, I thank you."

Puzzled, Nebet wondered if the girl was being sarcastic — or was she not as intelligent as Nebet had thought? "It is not necessary to thank me," she answered coolly. "It was her highness's wish to bring you and the wet nurse to the palace."

"Yes, of course, my lady," said the girl. "I mean, we wish to thank you for having cruel Steward Nakht removed from Sir Satepihu's estate."

Although taken aback, Nebet was adept at concealing her emotions. She asked casually, "Why do you — or your grandfather, for that matter — assume I had anything to do with that steward leaving?"

"Did you not, lady?" asked the girl, with an innocent glance from under her eyelashes. "My sister Leah, who is married to a gardener at the landlord's villa, told my Aunt Shiphrah that right after your visit to the landlord's wife, the landlord sent Steward Nakht to Nubia to supervise a silver mine. And the next thing the villagers knew, Steward Peneb was back."

Before Nebet could decide whether to confirm or deny this or simply reprimand the girl for impertinence, she — Mery — went on. "I would like to ask another favor, lady, a very small one. May I be excused from the dance practice?"

"For what reason?" asked Nebet, annoyed but also intrigued by the girl's boldness.

"The music master wishes me to take off my tunic, and I cannot do that. It is against the customs of my people. But I would gladly grind grain instead, or beat flax, or — "

"No one wants you to grind grain, silly girl," snapped Nebet. "We have slaves for that." She felt unreasonably irritated — with the Hebrew girl for presuming to say what she would and would not do, with the music master for failing to deal with the girl himself, and with herself for not knowing quite how to handle the problem. She hesitated, then went on, "Very well. You will practice the lute rather than dancing. Unless" — a note of sarcasm entered her voice — "the customs of your people forbid the playing of stringed instruments?"

"No, my lady," said the girl. "Thank you, my lady."

As the Hebrew girl bowed and drew back, Nebet regarded her thoughtfully. She had no standing at the palace — she was only a young servant, a newly arrived servant, and an unnecessary servant at that. Yet she had an air of dignity, as if some hidden strength was with her nevertheless.

After settling the details of the shrine to Osiris with the craftsmen, Nebet approached the princess. The conversation with the girl had reminded her that she needed to inform Bint-Anath of the understanding with Satepihu's wife. Otherwise, the princess would balk at her end of the bargain. This moment in the garden, when her highness was holding the baby, was a good time to bring up the subject.

"Satepihu's wife, sitting right next to us at the feast?" Princess Bint-Anath made a face at the baby, and he gurgled and waved his arms. "Oh, well. We can stand to be polite to that absurd woman for just one day, is that not so, Mose?"

"Your Highness has such wisdom," said Nebet, again concealing her surprise. She had expected the princess to protest more than that. Of course it was well that Bint-Anath joined in the scheme willingly. But Nebet hoped that she — she, Nebet, the best-informed and cleverest of any in the palace — was not beginning to lose her grasp.

CHAPTER 19

The Princess's Plans

One morning soon afterward, when Nebet appeared in Princess Bint-Anath's chamber as usual, the princess had already finished her bath. She was reclining on a couch while a maid touched up the tips of her toes and fingers with henna. The room seemed unusually peaceful — why? Gazing around, Nebet saw the parrot perched in a high window, quietly cracking seeds. Chi-Chi the monkey sat on the bed with his eyes closed, letting another maid comb his fur.

"I have been thinking, Nebet," said the princess. "I have been thinking it would be prudent to regain favor with some of the people I might have offended a bit. I wish to give a dinner party, a large one, and invite the Grand Vizier as guest of honor."

"The Grand Vizier?" Nebet had been thinking

about the Grand Vizier herself. For some time she had been pondering the question of how to mollify him. The best way, of course, *would* be for the princess to honor him. But Nebet would never have presumed to suggest that to Bint-Anath.

"A dinner party?" she went on, trying to hide her surprise. "A splendid idea! I will see that the invitation is delivered, Your Highness."

Later, Nebet had misgivings. Was Princess Bint-Anath only pretending to be prudent? Did she have a new prank to play on the Grand Vizier?

The night of the dinner party, Nebet watched from beyond the torchlight, in case there was some mischief she could head off. But the dinner was formal and dull enough to please the most pompous official. The high point of the evening was a song, specially composed by the music master at Nebet's order and sung by Princess Bint-Anath's musicians, about the vizier's accomplishments. Hardly daring to believe her eyes, Nebet saw the vizier's suspicious squint turn into a satisfied smile.

Nebet was pleased that the princess seemed to be mending her ways. Yet these attempts to behave properly could mean only one thing: Princess Bint-Anath was indeed determined to keep the Hebrew baby. If this was so, thought Nebet glumly, then she had better keep her promise to Taweret.

The next day, Nebet had the shrine of the hippopotamus goddess moved to an inconspicuous place in Princess Bint-Anath's garden, behind a clump of tamarisk bushes. Grudgingly, she set a bowl of dates in front of the goddess's statue. She hoped Taweret would understand (although hippos were not especially insightful) that she would deserve a *temple* only if the princess herself gave birth. Not for an adopted baby — and a Hebrew at that.

AS THE WEEKS went on, Nebet began to feel at loose ends. Half of her work had consisted of soothing the people Princess Bint-Anath had offended, or of blackmailing them if they were unwilling to be soothed. Also, Nebet was uneasy about the distance she now felt between Bint-Anath and herself.

Not that the princess was cool toward Nebet. In fact, she was kinder and more thoughtful than usual — she did not fly into fits of temper at her lady-in-waiting. But she did not fall into Nebet's arms to be comforted, either. In the past, the princess had usually been swayed by Nebet's suggestions. But when Nebet had tried to hint, two or three times, that the Hebrew girl showed no promise as a servant, the princess had coolly contradicted her. The other day Bint-Anath had remarked that Nebet was working too hard and might wish to take some time for herself. Nebet found that most disturbing.

And the princess no longer left all the planning to Nebet. One morning, when Nebet was attending the princess, a servant came from the King to summon his favorite daughter to play sennet with him in his favorite informal courtyard. Before Nebet could even make the suggestion, Bint-Anath gestured toward her jewelry chest. "I will wear my father's special gift, the golden duck pendant."

When Princess Bint-Anath returned from the King's quarters, her eyes were shining. "Nebet, my father (may he live and prosper) has agreed to attend the adoption ceremony!"

"The adoption ceremony of your — son?" Nebet was aware that it would be important to get the King's public approval for this adoption, but she had assumed it was too soon to broach the subject. "The King (may he live and prosper) committed himself to a ceremony two years away?"

"About two years, although the date is not yet certain," said Princess Bint-Anath. "He has ordered the astrologers to calculate a propitious time." While Nebet took this in, the princess continued, "It would also be proper for the Queen to lead the procession to the temple, would it not? But I am afraid I am in my mother's bad graces. Nebet, dear, will you watch for a chance for me to gain favor with her?"

At least I am still of *some* use to the princess, thought Nebet wryly. Inquiring among her sources, she soon learned that Queen Ystnefert was suffering from headaches again. So she sent Princess Bint-Anath's masseuse, the best in Pi-Rameses, to the Queen's suite to massage the royal temples. But Nebet took little satisfaction in coming up with such a simple idea. It was now Bint-Anath, not Nebet, who was planning two years ahead.

FOR THE FIRST few weeks, Nebet had not paid much attention to the Hebrew woman and girl, assuming that Bint-Anath's infatuation with the baby would fade and she would be able to convince the princess to send all three of them away. But now it was clear that Princess Bint-Anath was determined to keep and adopt this baby, and therefore the other two Hebrews would be harder to get out of the palace. Nebet felt uneasy — and irritated with herself. Long before this, she ought to have had a consultation with the servants' housekeeper about the princess's two new servants.

With the purpose of setting this matter straight, Nebet started one morning for the servants' quarters. Near the stables, a soldier leading a train of Libyan prisoners of war stopped to let her pass. Nebet glanced at the prisoners, shuffling in chains, their tattoos and their pointed beards smeared with dust and dried blood.

The border wars with the Libyans in the West seemed to be getting all the attention these days, Nebet mused. There was little talk about the menace from the East. And according to her sources, that last decree about Hebrew male babies was not being enforced by the estate-holders around Pi-Rameses. Perhaps word had gotten around among the stewards that Steward Nakht's zealousness had only won him banishment to Nubia.

At the servants' quarters, Nebet waited in the courtyard while the gatekeeper went to fetch the housekeeper. On the other side of the courtyard, the nurses chatted while their babies fed or napped. All except the Hebrew nurse, that is. She sat apart from the others, as out of place in her patterned wool tunic as an owl in a flock of white egrets. The girl Mery was nowhere in sight — of course not; she must be at music practice at this time of the morning.

The housekeeper bustled up to Nebet, bowing. The woman wore a brightly colored woven belt, Nebet noticed, of an unusual design. "My lady, what an honor! I was just overseeing the slaves who wash the babies' laundry, the lazy things." She was surprised when Nebet inquired about the Hebrew wet nurse and the girl. "Will they be staying much longer, lady? The girl is bright and helpful, but her mother does nothing but mope. And she drinks no beer, and she hardly speaks two words of Egyptian. Would not the child sent to her highness by Osiris be better off with an Egyptian nurse? Of course, her highness must know best."

Upon further questioning, Nebet learned that the Hebrews had been placed in the dancing girls' sleeping hall but had ended up sleeping in the courtyard for the first few nights. Fair-minded, Nebet did not allow herself to blame the housekeeper for what was her own fault. It was Nebet herself who had given the woman the impression that the Hebrews were only a passing whim of the princess.

What was intriguing was that the girl Mery had managed to get room for herself and her mother in the nurses' hall. The housekeeper did not exactly say that, of course. But putting this and that together, especially the housekeeper's new belt of Eastern weave, Nebet gathered that there had been an exchange of favors.

Nebet did not mention her conclusions to the housekeeper. She only said, "From now on, the wet nurse of the princess's child must drink a bowl of cow's milk every day — you may add it to Princess Bint-Anath's account. And you must keep an eye on the wet nurse to make sure her care of the baby is up to the palace standards."

On her way back to the princess's suite, Nebet reflected that it was almost time for the yearly royal procession up the river to Thebes. Did Princess Bint-Anath expect to bring the baby with her? Most likely. Nebet had better suggest to the princess that it would be wise to leave Mose at home in Pi-Rameses for a few weeks. In her newly sensible mood, Bint-Anath ought to understand: Better to keep the baby's obviously Hebrew nurse out of sight of the High Priest of Amon-Re.

Of course the High Priest's spies were here in Pi-Rameses, too. Nebet supposed that the baby, in himself, would not bring danger to Princess Bint-Anath and those who served her. And the wet nurse would not be noticed by the wrong people as long as she stayed in the servants' quarters. The servants' housekeeper, obligated to Nebet for her third son's acceptance in the scribes' school, kept her well informed, and Nebet felt confident that the Thebans had not yet placed any spies among the other servants.

The girl Mery, coming and going through the palace grounds every day as the princess had ordered, was more of a problem. Should Nebet keep on working to get Princess Bint-Anath to send her away? That would be the safest course. But Nebet had never come across a girl quite like this one. Against her better judgment, she was curious to see what kind of place Mery could make for herself in the world of the palace. She decided to wait — and watch.

CHAPTER 20

Miri's Song

מרים

It was not so bad, living in a palace.
Now that I was learning to play the lute rather
than trying to do high kicks in my Hebrew clothes, I
loved going to the music courtyard every morning.
While the dancing girls shook themselves and pos-
tured at one end of the courtyard, I joined a group
with the master lutist at the other end. At first I was
almost afraid to touch the lute they gave me. Its wood
was silky-smooth, inlaid with figures of song birds.

But when I began to pluck the strings, I forgot
about the way the lute looked. I heard — I *made!* —
notes, then notes and chords, twining into a melody.
Morning after morning, the music bore me away. As I
worked at learning to change chords or play a cascade
of notes, I would lose track of time. The shadows in
the courtyard would shorten and almost disappear,

and before I knew it we would be dismissed for the midday meal.

Each day, when I returned to the servants' quarters, *Imma* questioned me about what I had been doing all morning. At first I tried to explain what I was learning, but she could not understand how practicing an instrument could take all morning, every day except feast days. I felt she did not quite believe me. "It is what Lady Nebet wishes me to do," I said finally, and that seemed to make her angry, although she said no more.

After the midday rest, my mother would prepare Moshe for his afternoon with Princess Bint-Anath. She fed him and bathed him and wrapped him in fresh linen. I watched carefully as she wound the strips of cloth in a perfect pattern around his legs.

No need for *Imma* to know that the first thing the princess did was unwind the swaddling and dip the baby in the pool. "Paddle, my little duck," she laughed as he kicked his legs. I gathered up the linen strips as Princess Bint-Anath flung them aside, and then I retreated behind the olive trees. At the end of each afternoon, I carefully re-swaddled Moshe in the same pattern my mother had made.

For weeks I spent my afternoons in the garden simply keeping out of the way. Ladies, I learned, expect servants to be invisible, yet ready to turn visible instantly if my lady wants a cool drink or if monkey dung needs to be cleaned up. But most of the time, no one seemed to want me for anything in the garden. So I sat with my back against the trunk of an olive tree and watched and listened and breathed in the lotus-perfumed air.

Sometimes the princess's parrot perched nearby and talked to me. That is, it repeated remarks like, "Paddle, my little duck. Awk!" I had to put a hand over my mouth to smother my laughter.

The princess's striped cat might also wander over to me after it finished licking the goat's milk left over from Moshe's bowl. At first I was nervous about its sharp teeth and claws, but it only wanted to be scratched around its ears and whiskers. The cat was a gift to the princess, one of the other servants told me, from the main temple of the cat-goddess Bast at Bubastis.

I did not realize how much I looked forward to these hours in the garden until the princess and the rest of Pharaoh's household left for the New Year's festival in Thebes. Then I spent every afternoon — for three weeks — with *Imma* in the dusty servants' courtyard, with nothing to do but translate between her and Kawit, the kind woman who was wet nurse to the baby of one of the King's concubines. The most exciting parts of their conversations had to do with hand-loom patterns, or whether the babies were cutting teeth. By the time the court returned from Thebes, I was ready to bribe a slave to let me wash the babies' laundry.

ONE LAZY AFTERNOON in floodtime — the Egyptians call it *akhet* — I was sitting in the princess's garden under my usual olive tree, with the parrot perched nearby on a low branch. Princess Bint-Anath had already led her daily procession to her shrine to Osiris and offered a tray of painted duck eggs. Now she and her ladies lounged by the pool, while the servants took turns singing to them. I was thinking how beautiful and fascinating the garden was, and what a shame it was that *Imma* had never seen it. She could not appear while the princess was using the garden, of course. But perhaps no one would mind if I brought her here when the garden was empty?

The cat strolled over to me, its striped tail twitching. Its yellow eyes widened as it stared up at the parrot.

"Awk!" The parrot spread its wings and glared down at the cat. "Go back to Bubastis!"

I laughed out loud, forgetting that I was supposed to be invisible. A song had just ended, and the princess and her ladies looked in my direction. Princess Bint-Anath's smile made me wonder if she had taught the parrot that phrase herself.

Lady Nebet, on the other hand, gazed at me in a cool, measuring way. "Perhaps Your Highness would like to hear a song from the girl Mery," she said to the princess. "She has attended music practice for months now. Surely even a farmer's daughter could learn one song in a season."

Princess Bint-Anath gave a little nod, and Lady Nebet beckoned me. The servant who had just sung held out her lute. My stomach fluttered, but I took the instrument and strummed it, tuning the strings a bit. I was learning several songs at music practice, but they were complicated, in either the verses or the music, and I was not absolutely sure of any of them.

As I hesitated, Lady Nebet watched me closely, and it struck me that this was a test. I did not know why she would want to test me, but I would *not* fail. There was one Egyptian song I knew quite well, although I had not actually been taught it.

With a bold chord, I launched into a rollicking song that the dancing girls sang. It was about a lady mouse and her cat servants. The song made fun of the cats, but it was not very respectful of the aristocratic mice, either. As I ended the first verse, there was a shocked silence from Princess Bint-Anath's women. They all looked from me to the princess, except for Lady Nebet. A faint smile touched her lips, and she watched me with interest.

Then Princess Bint-Anath giggled. "How would you like *that*, Mose?" she asked the baby. "What if *you* were taken care of by cats?"

The other ladies laughed in relief — all except Lady Nebet, who glanced from the princess to me and back again. I sang the rest of the verses, each one more ridiculous than the last. After I had finished, the princess tucked a lotus behind the ear of her chief lady-in-waiting. "You did well to have the girl trained in music, Nebet dear. She must sing for us again."

Lady Nebet nodded her thanks, but she looked uncertain. It was not an expression I had ever seen on Lady Nebet's face.

CHAPTER 21

A Second Joseph?

מרים

When I asked the head gardener about bringing my mother to the princess's garden, he assured me there was nothing wrong with it, if we came very early in the morning or at midday. The garden was always deserted, except for servants, at those times. I thought *Imma* would be delighted at a chance to leave the servants' quarters, but she refused to go. "It is more fitting for me to stay here," she said, pulling her shawl over her head. "I wish they did not keep *you* out all afternoon. Although I suppose it is best that one of us watch over your baby brother."

I began to wonder if my mother enjoyed being unhappy. It made me restless to be around her; her only occupations now were tending to Moshe or weaving on her hand loom. At least I was able to use her weaving to make friends with the other servants. A beautiful belt for the housekeeper got us moved to the nurses' sleeping hall. A handsome headband for the gatekeeper assured that if our relatives visited, they would be allowed to enter the servants' quarters unquestioned.

Still, I did not spend time with *Imma* if I could help it. On days when the morning music practice ended early, instead of going straight back to our quarters, I began to explore the palace a bit.

There was always something interesting happening — or rather, many interesting things happening at once — in that small city that was the palace. I could eavesdrop on a classroom where the royal children were taught to read and write. I could watch a sculptor at work on yet another image of the King. I could visit the drill grounds, where Pharaoh's foot soldiers in leather helmets and shields might be training, their copper-bladed spears flashing in the sunlight.

One morning I found myself outside the entrance to the grand reception hall. Several guards stood outside the doorway, but I edged close enough to peer inside. The hall was a grove of carved and painted pillars, rows and rows of them, thicker and taller than date palms. The blue-green ceiling was so high above the floor that I could hardly see it in the dim light.

At the far end of the hall, a life-size statue of Pharaoh sat on a dais. The only light in the hall fell behind him. He wore the double crown of Upper and Lower Egypt, and he held his royal scepter and flail.

"Attention! Here comes the Canaanite ambassador," the captain warned his guards. They all straightened their spears and put on stern expressions. I turned to see a procession approaching along the arcade, men with long hair and full, curled beards. As they came closer, I could see that the foreign dignitaries were sweating in their heavy robes. The servants following the ambassador carried ornamented chests, full of tribute.

I knew, from *Sabba's* stories, that Canaan was a land beyond the Great Eastern Desert. Our ancestor Abraham had lived in Canaan at one time. But I had thought that most of the Canaanites were shepherds, with a few of them living in little towns. Not so. The ambassador and his men might be Pharaoh's subjects, but clearly they came from a large, rich city.

The procession halted at the doorway, and the royal guards motioned the Canaanite soldiers to leave their spears outside. Then the procession swept into the hall. The Canaanites walked more and more slowly, as if they were in awe of the majesty of the place.

The sitting statue rose. My stomach fluttered. This was no statue. It was Pharaoh himself.

The Canaanites fell on their knees before him. "He is only a man," I whispered to myself, repeating my grandfather's words. But my own knees shook as I crept away.

IMMA MIGHT have been happier at Pi-Rameses if she had been allowed to visit our family in the village once or twice a month. "If only I could go home, just

135

for a day!" she sighed one evening, as we sat in the courtyard after supper. Kawit, sitting nearby, asked me why my mother was sad.

Kawit listened sympathetically as I explained in Egyptian that *Imma* had not left our village since she was married, and she was homesick. "Poor Djochabed! But a wet nurse cannot leave the palace. We are paid to be here with the babies. And of course Princess Bint-Anath would not let Mose's wet nurse take him along on a visit to her village!"

"Never mind, *Imma*," I told my mother. "Soon I will go home for a visit and get all the news for you." Then I translated my remark for Kawit. I often made my remarks twice, once in Hebrew and once in Egyptian, when I was around the two of them. This was becoming increasingly tiresome — sometimes I felt like the princess's parrot. I was beginning to think that my mother might make more of an effort to learn Egyptian.

"Leave the palace to visit your village?" Kawit looked shocked. "You had better not let Lady Nebet hear you talking like that! It would sound ungrateful — you might even be dismissed. After all, your family can visit you here."

"But they are tenant farmers!" I protested. "It is very hard for them to get leave from their work in the fields or brickyards." Still, I remembered Lady Nebet's calculating look the first time I sang for the princess. I could not afford to give her an excuse to dismiss me. Moshe, and especially my mother, needed me here.

So in spite of having more time for leisure than we

136

had ever dreamed of, *Imma* and I had to wait for the family to visit us. I had missed the first visit — Aunt Shiphrah and Tamar — because they arrived in the afternoon, when I was in the garden with Princess Bint-Anath. When *Imma* told me the news afterward, I was so disappointed that tears came to my eyes. It was as if I were allowed only one meal a week, and I had just missed it.

A MONTH OR SO later, I came back from music practice to find two men, one middle-aged and one gray-haired, sitting with my mother in the servants' courtyard. *"Sabba!"* I shouted joyfully, running toward them. *"Abba!"* Then I stopped short, badly frightened. *"Abba,* you did not report for work-crew duty,* I whispered. What would the steward do to him when he found out?

"Did your Aunt Shiphrah not tell you that Steward Nakht is gone?" asked my father, with one of his rare grins.

"Yes," I said, "but still — "

"And Peneb is so thankful to be steward again," my grandfather added, "it takes only a duck egg or two to bribe him." He made a sly gesture behind his back, as if he were slipping the steward an egg.

Imma and I laughed out loud. My mother's face was alight in a way I had not seen since we left the village. Proudly she showed my father and grandfather the sacks of wheat, her payment as nurse to the princess's baby, that she had been saving for them.

137

They gazed greedily at the sacks of grain. My father and grandfather were *scrawny*, I realized. Although I was happy to see them, I was taken aback by their appearance. They were dressed in their festival tunics, but even these clothes looked shabby to me.

As we shared our midday meal with them, *Sabba* told the story of Steward Nakht's dismissal. I was happy to listen to my grandfather's mellow storytelling voice at first, but as he went on and on I began to shift impatiently. I had already heard this story from *Imma*, who had heard it from Aunt Shiphrah, and of course my father had even heard *Sabba* tell it before. Yet my mother and father were nodding and smiling as if they could never get tired of it.

Also, I could not agree with the way my grandfather described one of the people in the story — Lady Nebet.

As *Sabba* told it, she was a kind Egyptian noblewoman who was indignant at Steward Nakht's treatment of our clan. From what I had seen of Lady Nebet so far, she was practical, reasonable, fair — but not a person who would be kind to strangers. And she had looked so surprised when I thanked her, as if it had not occurred to her that having Steward Nakht sent away would benefit us.

After *Sabba* finished his story with his usual flourish, *Abba* and *Imma* went off to a quiet corner of the courtyard, while *Sabba* settled himself in the shade of the fig tree. "Unh!" he groaned. "It feels as if there were pebbles in my joints." I sat down at his feet, cradling Moshe. The baby waved his arms and made faces at his grandfather.

Sabba nodded thoughtfully at him. "I believe it is coming clear." He was talking to me but still looking at the baby. "Yes, I have been mystified for some time. Why did the Lord choose such a roundabout way to save this child? Then it struck me: the Lord must have a special purpose for him."

"A special purpose?" I glanced down at my baby brother. He was trying to get his fist to his mouth, but he kept punching himself in the cheek.

"Have you not dreamed about it?" *Sabba* leaned forward, speaking in a low voice. "I thought perhaps the Gift would reveal Moshe's destiny to you. For I believe that this child is destined to become a second Joseph."

"I have had no special dreams," I answered.

"No dreams?" *Sabba*'s bushy eyebrows shot up, then pulled together in a frown. "Have you practiced keeping an open spirit? For you cannot receive guidance without openness. Water does not flow into the fields through a blocked ditch."

I did not like being compared to a ditch, and a blocked one at that. "There has been much to do at the palace," I murmured vaguely. "*Imma* leaves everything to me. But I will try. . . ."

My grandfather gave me a searching look, but then, to my relief, he went back to talking of Moshe and God's purpose for him.

I realized what I had said was true. I had been so busy with my new life that I had not thought to wonder why God had saved Moshe.

Now, as my grandfather explained it, it made

sense. The Hebrews in Egypt had no power, because we were all tenant farmers. We needed a protector among the Egyptians, one as powerful as Prince Joseph had been. As the princess's adopted son, Moshe would have that power.

"When Moshe is a man," declared *Sabba*, "he will cause the cruel laws against Hebrews to be thrown in the fire. He will be heir to the princess's lands — we will own farms again!"

As *Sabba* talked, I imagined our Lord Moshe, lofty and stern, in his pleated kilt, a collar of precious stones and gold beads adorning his neck. He raised one hand to make a proclamation, while rows of slaves and servants and minor officials crouched before him.

I looked down at Moshe again. Although he was growing and now had a thick head of hair, he was still only a baby. He smiled his adorable dimpled smile — and drooled.

CHAPTER 22

Mery

*A*khet — floodtime — passed, and again *peret* — the growing season — and Nebet was no closer than before to deciding what to do about the Hebrew girl, Miri. "Miri" was her Hebrew name, Nebet had learned, but ladies and servants alike had already gotten into the habit of calling her by the Egyptian name of "Mery." The princess often asked her to sing for them in the garden. The girl had a natural talent for music, Nebet had to admit, and a lively way of performing. She was clearly intelligent, and she seemed sincerely devoted to the baby Mose, which of course pleased Princess Bint-Anath.

Early one afternoon, when the girl brought Mose to the princess, her highness motioned her to stay instead of backing off into the olive trees. "See, I have a basket of toys for Mose. Which do you think he will prefer?"

At the princess's invitation, Mery helped her take the toys from the basket one by one and present them to the baby. He especially liked a brown pottery lion, with jaws that opened and closed. Bint-Anath pretended to roar like a lion each time she opened the creature's mouth, and the baby squealed. "*You* are a little lion, with that mane," she told him, ruffling his shaggy hair.

"See what he thinks of the mirror," suggested Nebet. Mery obediently took a bronze hand-mirror from the basket and held it up for the baby. He stared at his own image in the shiny surface and pointed, grunting, "Uh."

"Yes, see the *baby*, Mose," said Nebet. Her son Inyotef, at about this age, had tried to imitate words. "Say 'baby.' "

"Uh," said Mose, pointing again.

Princess Bint-Anath seized the baby's finger and kissed it. "He is too little to talk, is that not so, Mose darling?"

Putting the mirror back into the basket, the girl remarked, as if to herself, "But Aaron could say many words when — " She stopped and bit her lip.

"Who is 'Aaron,' pray tell?" asked the princess carelessly. "And what has he to do with my child?"

"Nothing, Your Highness," said Mery with lowered eyes. "Aaron is my brother. I spoke foolishly, for he has nothing to do with Prince Mose."

Nothing, except that Mose also is her brother, thought Nebet. She had long suspected that was why the girl had been watching his basket from the reeds that fateful day about a year ago. And it followed that the Hebrew woman was Mose's mother as well as Mery's.

Glancing discreetly at Princess Bint-Anath, Nebet wondered if she had guessed the truth. If so, she seemed determined to ignore it. She waved Mery away and lifted Mose to stand on her knees. "Did you save a kiss for your mother? Ooh, look, I see a kiss right *there!*" Bint-Anath dived at the child's neck and nuzzled him, and he laughed and squirmed.

AFTER THAT, Nebet could not help seeing a certain family resemblance between Mery and Mose. Not a startling resemblance — just a likeness in the set of their eyes, and a dimple in the same place when they smiled. But Nebet decided to take steps to make Mose look as Egyptian as possible.

"Does it seem to Your Highness that Prince Mose's hair grows long?" she asked the princess one morning, after they had discussed the schedule for the feast day commemorating the King's great victory over the Hittites. "Shall I summon the hairdresser to the garden this afternoon?"

"Yes, it would be wise to cut his hair," agreed Princess Bint-Anath. "It hangs down his neck and makes him fretful in this hot season."

Nebet rather expected the baby to fuss when his hair was cut, but he hardly squirmed at all as the hairdresser, Senen, clipped around his head. He laughed as she dipped him into the pool to wash off the itchy bits of hair, water streaming from his one long sidelock.

Happening to glance in Mery's direction, Nebet looked again. The girl was nervously clenching her hands. So, it disturbs her that his hair is cut, thought Nebet.

That evening, just before sunset, Nebet stopped by the servants' quarters to inquire about one of her maids, who had been ill. As the housekeeper rose from her supper to greet the lady-in-waiting, Nebet's eye was caught by the Hebrew woman. She was feeding bits of bread to Mose, who toddled away a few steps, then toddled back for another bite. But the woman's attention was not on the child, but on her, Nebet. She was glaring at her as if she hated her.

Nebet ignored the wet nurse, but she did not forget that look. The next afternoon in the garden, she seated herself under a jasmine arbor and beckoned to Mery. "I noted yesterday evening that the Hebrew woman was distressed," she said. "Do you know why?"

The girl looked distressed herself. She opened her mouth, then closed it. She tried again: "Because . . . because she does not . . ."

"Speak!" ordered Nebet.

The girl sighed. "She does not like the way Mose's hair was cut."

Nebet gave a short laugh. "Indeed! A wet nurse criticizes one of the most skilled hairdressers in the palace?"

"She did not criticize the hairdresser's skill, lady,"

144

said the girl in a low voice. "She only thought the baby's hair looked very — very — "

"Well?" Nebet could guess what the Hebrew woman's objection was, but she was curious to see how Mery would explain it.

" — Egyptian," whispered Mery. She cleared her throat and added, "I explained to her that it was *better* for Mose to look — "

" — Egyptian," said Nebet dryly. "Since he is, after all, an Egyptian prince." So that was why Mery had looked disturbed when Mose's hair was cut. She had known that her mother (Mose's real mother, after all) would be unhappy.

Later, observing Mery playing a board game with one of the ladies, Nebet reflected that the girl understood a great deal for one so young. She seemed to have a sense for what favors she might ask for herself or her family, and what things, though disturbing, must be borne. In fact, she seemed to have a much better sense of this than her mother.

THE INCIDENT gave Nebet an idea about Mery herself. All this time Nebet had assumed she should get rid of the Hebrew girl, thinking her a danger to Princess Bint-Anath and her people. But truly, it was only Mery's appearance that was a danger.

If the girl dressed her hair in the Egyptian style and exchanged her striped wool tunic for a linen shift, Nebet thought, she would look no more Hebrew than Mose. She learned quickly, and she was becoming a favorite of the princess. Both these things made her valuable in Nebet's eyes. Instead of trying to have her dismissed, why not make use of her?

The next morning, Nebet took a linen shift from a storage chest and sent a slave to the servants' quarters to give it to Mery. The shift was plain, but of good-quality, newly loomed cloth. That afternoon, however, Mery appeared in the garden wearing her Hebrew clothes and carrying the linen garment over her shoulder. After presenting Mose to the princess, she knelt before Nebet.

"Did you not understand," asked Nebet sharply, "that you were to wear the linen shift?"

"My lady is more than kind to offer this servant such a fine garment," murmured the girl. "I deeply regret that I cannot wear it. It is not the custom of my clan to wear sheer cloth."

"Indeed." Nebet felt a flash of anger, and her first impulse was to order Mery to wear the Egyptian shift or be punished for disobedience. A servant had no right to refuse the request of Princess Bint-Anath's chief lady-in-waiting, especially such a reasonable request. But the anger faded almost immediately, crowded out of Nebet's mind by an intriguing thought. She turned from Mery without further discussion and clapped for a slave to take the shift back to storage.

Though outwardly calm, Nebet felt a little thrill of excitement, the thrill she always felt when a challenge presented itself. Clearly the Hebrew woman had forbidden her daughter to don Egyptian dress. Very well;

Nebet would arrange things so that Mery herself would decide to disobey her mother.

Nebet put on a bland expression and joined the women at the pool. Dropping a remark here and a question there, sprinkling bits of tantalizing rumor, she started the group talking about the next New Year's trip to Thebes. Soon they were all chattering about the adventures of the journey up the river, and the sights to be seen in Thebes, and their costumes for the ceremonies.

With satisfaction, Nebet noted that Mery seemed to be listening eagerly. Naturally, a spirited girl like Mery would long to accompany the princess to Thebes. Good. Nebet would let Mery long for a few days, then suggest the idea to the princess.

In fact, it was Princess Bint-Anath who brought up the idea at one of their morning planning sessions. "If only my Mose could come to Thebes with me!" She was stretched out on a couch to let her masseuse rub scented oil into her shoulders. "But the child thrives with his Hebrew nurse, and of course *she* cannot be brought to Thebes."

"Of course," agreed Nebet, "although it is a pity." She opened her mouth to mention the girl, but the princess spoke again.

"That girl Mery is dear, is she not? So fresh, so entertaining. I will miss her, too."

Nebet smiled inwardly. "She sings well," she agreed, "and her Egyptian accent is almost perfect. It is really only her Hebrew dress that makes her . . . unsuitable to accompany Your Highness to Thebes."

"Exactly!" Princess Bint-Anath rose suddenly to her knees on the couch, while the masseuse snatched the jar of scented oil before it could spill. "How well you see things, Nebet. Let the girl Mery be provided with Egyptian dress, then, and prepared for the journey."

ONE EVENING the following week, when Princess Bint-Anath was leading the priestesses in rites at the temple of Set, Nebet summoned the Hebrew girl. After Mery had knelt in front of her chair and bowed, Nebet gave her a gracious smile. "You may sit. You may have some fruit." She gestured to the platter of grapes and figs on a nearby table.

"Thank you, my lady." The girl politely took a grape and waited.

"Let us speak frankly," said Nebet, "for you are an intelligent girl, and you keep your eyes open and notice what goes on around you. I have a proposal that will be very much to your advantage, but you must choose to cooperate."

"Yes, my lady," was all Mery said, but she sat up straighter. Although it was difficult to read her expression in the lamplight, Nebet felt the time was right.

"Princess Bint-Anath is pleased with you," Nebet went on, "and she wishes to bring you along on the trip to Thebes. But although she is the favorite daughter of Pharaoh (may he live and prosper), she cannot openly defy the High Priest of Amon-Re. Do you know about the High Priest?"

"They say, my lady, that he is one of the most powerful men in Upper and Lower Egypt."

Nebet nodded. "Very good. Do they say anything else?"

Even in the dim light, Nebet could see Mery flinch. The girl answered, "That he hates Hebrews, my lady."

"They say correctly," said Nebet in an even tone. "Furthermore, he has spies working for him, even in Pi-Rameses. I would not be surprised if he arranged to place one of them on the princess's own barge.

"And so, if you are to accompany Princess Bint-Anath to the New Year's celebration at Thebes, you must appear to be an Egyptian. Now" — Nebet held up a hand — "I understand all about your customs. We must both compromise a bit. You must wear a white linen shift rather than your wool tunic. On the other hand, you will not be required to publicly worship Amon-Re. I can easily find some business to keep you away during the ceremonies."

The girl raised her eyes wonderingly to Nebet. "My lady is very considerate." She hesitated, then asked, "Will Prince Mose and his wet nurse also travel to Thebes?"

"No," answered Nebet, smiling inwardly at the unspoken part of the question. "The housekeeper tells me that the Hebrew nurse speaks little Egyptian, and from what I have seen of her, I doubt she would be willing to put aside her Hebrew dress."

"No, my lady," murmured Mery in a tone of relief.

"That is settled, then." Nebet made a gesture of

dismissal. "As I say, you have found favor in her highness's eyes. If you are as sensible and bright as I believe you are, then you can expect to go far at Pi-Rameses."

CHAPTER 23

Into the Heart of Egypt

מרים

By the time I returned from Lady Nebet's chambers, my mother and Moshe were fast asleep in the nurses' hall. I lay awake on my mat for a time, listening to the breathing of the women and babies, watching the stars move across the high windows, and thinking about the trip up the river to Thebes. This year, I would not stay behind. But if *Imma* forbade me to go? I would not listen. I would *not* stay behind.

The next morning, as we ate breakfast in the courtyard, I told my mother that Princess Bint-Anath wanted me to go to Thebes with her entourage, to entertain the ladies with singing and lute-playing. "Lady Nebet understands that I will not worship their god Amon-Re, even at the great festival," I added quickly. I said nothing of my agreement to dress as an Egyptian.

I expected an argument, but *Imma* did not even question me closely. "A girl your age, alone among heathen for three weeks? Aiy! Well, I suppose it may not be for ill, as long as you say the prayers." A tear trickled down her face and dropped onto Moshe's close-cropped head. "For three weeks I will be without companionship, merely so that the princess may have another musician."

I glanced sideways at Kawit, who was politely pretending not to wonder what we were talking about. "But Kawit will remain here."

"I mean, no one will speak to me in my own tongue."

I thought even this was not fair, since Kawit had made an effort to learn Hebrew words and phrases to help my mother feel more at home. "*Shalom*, peace," she said to my mother every morning.

"And I must dwell here like one in prison," *Imma* went on, "while our clan gathers for the shearing festival, and they celebrate the wedding of Tamar — such a good, dear girl! Oh, that you also were betrothed!"

"Tamar's wedding, already?" I started, for it had slipped my mind. I would not be at my cousin's wedding, either. I would not sing and dance with the other girls.

I was sorry to miss the shearing festival and Tamar's wedding. But I realized I was not sorry that there was no chance of my becoming betrothed this year. Nor was I sorry to leave my mother, with her spells of listlessness and gloom. Guiltily, I thought that the day of the departure for Thebes could not come too quickly for me.

ON THAT DAY, before dawn, one of Lady Nebet's slaves brought me to a storage room in the princess's suite. She helped me change from my striped tunic into a linen sheath. At once I felt the comfort of the air flowing through the weave of the light fabric; at this time of year, the end of the harvest season, heat lingered in the brick walls even overnight.

The slave held out jewelry for me: a necklace of rows of copper and shell beads, a copper arm band, copper rings for my fingers and toes. She combed lotus-scented oil into my curls.

At first I felt self-conscious in my new clothes, half-expecting someone to say, "Look, Mery has dressed up as an Egyptian girl." But no one paid any attention to me, for the whole palace was bustling with the final preparations for boarding the royal fleet. Only Lady Nebet, looking over the servants who were coming along to Thebes, fastened her glance on me for a moment. Her lips curved slightly, reminding me of the cat after it finished the goat's milk.

Following the princess's retinue to the docks, I watched the royal barges set sail up the river in stately procession. First the King's barge, of course; then Queen Ystnefert's, and then those of the lesser wives in order of importance. With the swelling of each sail, I drew a deeper breath into my lungs.

Now it was the turn of the grown princes and princesses to join the procession. Princess Bint-Anath's ship was one of the first to cast off from the docks, and I let out my breath in relief. Without realizing it, I had feared that my mother would find a way to stop me, at the last moment, from taking this journey.

But I was on my way to Thebes! The other servants and I were put to work, first adjusting the awning so that the ladies were comfortably shaded, and then serving them cakes and cool drinks. As Lady Nebet took a cup from me, she nodded toward a woman I had not seen before. "Make sure you serve Lady Tetisheri of Thebes next," she said, with a slight emphasis on the place name. "She is our special guest."

I tried to keep my expression as bland as Lady Nebet's, but I remembered what she had said about a spy for the High Priest of Amon-Re on the princess's ship. Lady Tetisheri was a plump woman with little hands and feet. She laughed a great deal and touched the other ladies on the arm as she talked.

Busy with my duties, I could not observe the passing scene on the river as I wished. But I noticed that all along the banks, people clustered to watch the royal procession. Princess Bint-Anath raised a hand now and then in gracious greeting.

As we passed the dock of a villa, something about the shape of the guard tower and the treetops above the walls struck me as familiar. I heard the princess remark to Lady Nebet, as she waved to the crowd on the dock, "What a shame that I could not find a place for Satepihu's wife on my barge."

Lady Nebet laughed, and I knew the princess was joking. But I had an odd feeling. If this was Sir Satepihu's villa, then we had already passed the canal that led to my village. For the first time in weeks, I imagined what my clan would be doing.

It was almost floodtime, so they would be preparing for the rising waters. They would be hauling their boats to the top of the canal banks. They would hasten to cut a last harvest of papyrus before the swollen river drowned the reeds.

A painful aching in my throat took me by surprise. Just for a moment, I missed my people. I wished the royal fleet were instead the fleet of the clan of Levi, all of us launched on an adventure together.

DAY AFTER DAY went by, and the Nile River unwound under the prow of Princess Bint-Anath's barge. We set sail each morning after breakfast, and stopped each evening as guests at some villa or other. On the barge, the princess and her ladies had even more idle time than usual, and all the servants, even Princess Bint-Anath's hairdresser, were called upon to entertain. I did not want to sing over and over the few songs I had learned in music practice, and of course the ladies would not understand Hebrew songs, so I began making up my own.

I was delighted to find that music seemed to attract stories, the way flowers draw bees to their nectar. As I plucked out a melody on my lute, Senen the hairdresser, curling a lady's tresses, might begin talking as if to herself. "Before we were married, my husband went off with Pharaoh in the division of Set, to fight the Hittites. For months, there was no news. I paid for an oracle at the temple of Amon-Re, but it told me nothing. I feared my beloved was dead!" With a little description, and some "Ohs!" and "Ahs!" I could stretch out that story into four or five verses.

Likewise, each story seemed to call forth a certain rhythm and melody. All of *Sabba*'s stories — the animal fables, the account of how the wicked city of Gomorrah was destroyed, the story of why Adam and Eve were banished from the Garden of Eden — were easy to put to music. If I began saying the story out loud, more or less in *Sabba*'s words, as I strummed chords, the story and the music would begin to grow together into a single harmonious thing. I loved this work — if it could be called work.

One afternoon, as the ladies lounged on cushions under the striped awning, Princess Bint-Anath commanded, "Sing us a new ballad, Mery."

I had hoped she would ask me, because I had just finished composing a song about my favorite story, "Prince Joseph." It made a good long ballad, winding like a river from Joseph's boyhood, beyond the Eastern Desert, all the way to his princehood in Egypt. As I sang, the princess listened raptly, and I was so caught up in the story myself that I was shocked when Lady Nebet interrupted. I had just gotten to an exciting part — when Joseph is brought out of the dungeon to interpret Pharaoh's dream.

It happened that I was looking in Lady Nebet's direction at that moment, although everyone else was looking at me as I sang. The head lady-in-waiting was sitting on the edge of the barge beside Lady Tetisheri. I was startled to see Lady Nebet grasp a line, to anchor herself, and then lean suddenly backward with one arm flung out. The "special guest" from Thebes fell into the river as easily as a frog plopping into a canal.

"Alas!" screamed Lady Nebet, as if she had not caused the accident, "Give aid!" All the ladies jumped up, exclaiming and gawking, as a guard hurried to reach out one of the long oars so the victim could seize it, and the crew labored to bring the ship around. I jumped up too, but Lady Nebet gripped me by the arm and steered me to the other side of the barge.

"You are not to finish that song, no matter how many times Princess Bint-Anath asks you!" she hissed. "You must say that was the last verse. You must think of another song, something quite different, to distract her."

Her expression was so fierce, I wondered if her mind had been touched by the sun. "I d-do not understand," I stammered.

"Ignorant girl! Do you wish to be questioned by the High Priest's guards about your treasonous story?" I must have looked stupid, because she gave my arm a shake. "Obviously, this 'Djo-sef' of your song lived at the time when the Hyksos, invaders from the East, occupied the Delta. How else could an Easterner have risen to power? It was a black time for Egyptians! That shameful history is behind the High Priest's campaign against Hebrews."

157

I was cold with fear, but I was also curious. This fit together with what *Sabba* had always said about the old days, and I wanted to know more. But Lady Nebet dropped her hand from my arm and drew herself up. "There is no need for me to explain myself to a servant. Do as I say."

By this time the crew had pulled Lady Tetisheri back into the barge. Lady Nebet rushed over to the Theban woman with apologies, vowing to replace an earring lost in the river, drying her off with her own embroidered stole. The continued confusion gave me time to collect my wits.

When Princess Bint-Anath again settled herself on the cushions and bade me go on, I had decided on another song. I had not sung it so far because I had doubts about it, but I thought Lady Nebet would approve of it. Trying not to look at Lady Tetisheri or to imagine what it would be like to be questioned by the High Priest's men, I plucked the lute with trembling fingers.

My song was a lullaby that told how a heron, poking in the mud along the river, found a gold pendant shaped like a duck. The heron brought the pendant, dangling from his long bill, to the god Osiris, and Osiris recognized it as the one Princess Bint-Anath had lost. Pitying the princess, the god placed the pendant around the neck of a perfect baby. He put the baby in a basket — and guided the basket down the Nile to the princess's bathing place.

When I began the song, a surprised frown appeared on the princess's face. I pretended not to notice, but I was afraid she would interrupt and demand the rest of the ballad of Joseph. However, at the first mention of the gold pendant, her forehead smoothed, and she seemed to forget about the other song.

As I strummed the last chord, Princess Bint-Anath clapped and laughed and wiped away a tear. "How much I miss my little son!" Lady Nebet gave me the smallest nod — she was pleased, too.

But I was troubled. The idea for this song had come to me some time ago, before we left for Thebes. I thought of it one afternoon in the garden, watching Princess Bint-Anath play with Moshe. The verses came to me easily, one after another, and I knew the princess would like it. But I had never sung it.

Now I imagined my clan standing behind the ladies, listening silently as I sang my lying song, sang praises to a heathen god. I was deeply ashamed.

CHAPTER 24

An Egyptian Girl

מרים

The north wind that carried us up the river seemed also to be pushing out the boundaries of the world. Late one afternoon, I said to Princess Bint-Anath's hairdresser, Senen, "Surely we will reach Thebes tomorrow?"

Senen smiled, not unkindly. "The day *after* the day after tomorrow. Does this seem like a far journey to you? My husband, who works for a trader, has traveled more than twice as far — all the way to Kush, at the southern border of the Empire."

"Then that is the source of the river, in Kush?" I wondered out loud.

Senen smiled again. "Not at all. The river flows from a source far beyond Kush, in an unknown land." She looked at me with her head to one side, studying me, then beckoned me to sit beside her.

160

"Let me touch up your eyes a bit with kohl, just to see the effect."

I sat down obediently, but my thoughts were on the world, which seemed to have grown much larger since we set off for Thebes. If Egypt was so much vaster than I had imagined, how far away could the land of my ancestors be? My mind would not stretch to that distance.

Senen took out the cosmetics box she used for the ladies, opened a pot of kohl, and outlined my right eye with a cosmetic stick. "There. Now the other eye — yes, fetching!"

Three days later, as we finally approached the docks of the King's palace in Thebes, I was astounded to see how much bigger Thebes was than Pi-Rameses. Of course I knew Thebes was an important city, but seeing for myself what that meant was something else. I suppose I had pictured a cluster of a few buildings and people: the temple of Amon-Re with its priests, and Lady Tetisheri and her household, and . . . not much more.

True to her word, Lady Nebet arranged for me to be absent from the week-long celebration. While the rest of Princess Bint-Anath's attendants witnessed the processions and ceremonies, and sang and danced and feasted, I oversaw the slaves who starched and ironed the garments and polished the jewelry for the next day's festivities. But they needed no overseeing, and I was bored and lonely. I whispered my Hebrew prayers and crept around the palace.

Unlike the palace at Pi-Rameses, the one at Thebes

seemed to have been built a long time ago. Some of the lesser gardens were overgrown, and in places the paint was flaking away from the elaborate scenes on the walls. The chambers were furnished with richly carved chairs and beds and chests, but the fine wood of the pieces was dull with scratches and dust.

Many of the old paintings on walls and pillars and the backs of chairs showed the god Amon-Re, crowned with a gilded sun-disc. I could see that in some murals, where there was room, an artist had taken fresh paint and squeezed in the figures of King Rameses and his patron goat-headed god, Set. And in one hall, lined with a row of statues of Amon-Re, a row of brightly painted statues of Pharaoh, wearing his ceremonial beard and double crown, had been placed against the opposite wall. They were only statues, but I wondered how they felt about a Hebrew girl staring boldly at them, without even bowing her head. The notion came into my head that if the two rows strode toward each other, they could crush me like a beetle. I left that hall quickly.

I WAS DELIGHTED, at the end of the celebration, to join the princess's retinue on a trip to the desert on the west side of the river. First we crossed the Nile on the barge, then took skiffs up a canal to the edge of the farmland. Then, with the princess and her ladies in canopied litters and the rest of us on foot, we climbed into the dry hills. I was surprised when we came to a walled village in this barren place, but Senen explained that these villagers were not farmers.

162

They were stonemasons and sculptors and painters who worked on the tombs of the pharaohs.

Senen also pointed out a wall of cliffs rising to the northwest. "The Valley of the Kings (may they live and prosper in the next world)." She had visited it with the princess a few years ago. There was a magnificent temple, she said, with towering columns and sphinxes and standing statues greater than any in the Delta, where King Rameses could be worshipped after he died. And this was but one structure in a whole city built for the dead kings.

On this trip, however, Princess Bint-Anath wished to inspect the progress on her own tomb, in the Valley of the Queens. So we followed her litter southwest from the workers' village, into the rocky desert, with the glaring sun above and the baking hot rocks underfoot. The portico of the princess's tomb was a welcome sight, and we hurried into its shade.

Inside, the cool was even more welcome. I paused to gaze at the scenes on the walls, carved in relief and painted in shades of reddish-brown and gold and blue-green, as well as black and white. By now, I could recognize many of the Egyptian gods. Hathor, Queen of Heaven, was always beautiful, always crowned with long, slender horns. Here she took Princess Bint-Anath by the hand to welcome her into the afterlife.

I also recognized Anubis, the jackal-headed god in the next panel. He set a pair of scales as Maat, goddess of justice, prepared to weigh the princess's heart against an ostrich feather. These ideas about what happened to the soul after death had seemed ridiculous to me when Kawit first explained them, but they were familiar to me now. The paintings were very life-like — too lifelike, I thought, in spite of their fantastical blending of human and animal in the figures of the gods. As if from very long ago and far away, I remembered the feeling of my visions. A feeling of closeness to a breathtaking Power, more intense than anything in everyday life.

I heard Senen whisper to one of the maids, "They say the artists have finished the murals in the main chamber. Now we will see who is truly in favor!"

I did not understand what she meant until we entered the next chamber, a spacious room with a vaulted ceiling. Shafts in the rock let in sunlight, so that we needed no lamps or torches to see the paintings that covered the walls. The master craftsman bowed and waved a hand at his work.

Senen nudged the maid, pointing to the nearest wall. This painted scene showed the princess in her chamber, where a hairdresser reached out an ivory pick to arrange her curls. A maid held up a robe ready for Princess Bint-Anath to slip on, and a lady-in-waiting lifted a pendant from a jewelry chest.

Princess Bint-Anath was really almost as beautiful as the princess in the painting. But the servants and the lady-in-waiting seemed to have grown slimmer and prettier in the afterlife. Still, anyone could recognize the hairdresser as Senen, the maid as Senen's friend, and the lady-in-waiting as Lady Nebet. The two servants beamed at each other, and Lady Nebet allowed herself a quiet smile.

164

"See, Nebet, how well the garden has turned out." The princess was admiring another wall. "Just as I ordered: my monkey picking dates, my parrot teasing the cat, and my ducks eating cake from my hands."

The ladies murmured compliments, but I was sure they were jostling each other not to see the pets but to find out which of them were pictured in the garden. Lady Nebet had been painted beside the princess, of course, handing her pieces of cake to toss to the ducks. Nearby, a girl I did not recognize knelt under a palm tree, strumming a lute.

As I peered at the painting more closely, a meaningful cough from Lady Nebet made me glance around. All the ladies were looking at me. "What a fine likeness of Mery, Your Highness," said Lady Nebet.

Mery? Me? The picture of myself that I carried in my head looked quite different: like my cousin Tamar, only a little younger. But this girl in the garden looked quite Egyptian, except perhaps for her long, unruly hair, and a glimpse of a bright sash in the folds of her linen shift.

Lady Nebet nodded at me, her eyes glowing. She was *proud* of me. I was as touched by her look as I was by the princess's favor. "O King's daughter, most gracious princess," I murmured with bowed head. "I do not deserve this honor."

As I raised my head, I saw some of the other servants exchanging sour glances, as if they agreed with me. But Lady Nebet said, "A charming touch, Your Highness."

The princess smiled at me and led the way deeper into her tomb.

CHAPTER 25

A Dream and a Message

מרים

During the journey home to Pi-Rameses, the mood was relaxed. The Egyptians seemed to feel that the New Year, launched by the proper ceremonies, had begun well. It was floodtime again, and the river was swollen, but not raging, with floodwater. The harvest would be good. Listening to the ladies and servants talking about the festivities in Thebes — the splendid ceremonies, the amazing entertainments, and the banquets — I wondered if I could not have attended them, only *pretending* to bow to Amon-Re.

On the last day of the journey back to Pi-Rameses, the princess beckoned me to follow her to the stern of the barge. She handed me a bottle of precious oil and ordered me to rub her arms and neck, as her ladies-in-waiting often did. "Work slowly," she told me. "We can speak freely here, for the wind carries our words upstream. I wish to know more of your Djo-sef."

I almost dropped the onyx bottle. "Lady Nebet — "

"Yes, yes; Nebet is worried about the High Priest's spies, even though Lady Tetisheri is safely back in Thebes." The princess stretched out the other arm for me to oil. "Perhaps there are still spies on my ship, ready to report anything they hear about Hebrews. But they cannot hear us downwind in the stern, and neither can Nebet."

My heart beat faster, and I was sure this was a moment of opportunity. But opportunity for what? "What do you wish to know about Joseph, Your Highness?" I asked cautiously.

"Djo-sef interpreted dreams, yes?"

"Yes, Your Highness, with the help of — "

She interrupted me with a wave of her hand. "So you believe this story of your ancestors?"

I nodded.

"There are many who call themselves interpreters of dreams," she continued, her eyes searching mine, "but I have never known any whose interpretations could be relied on."

"Yes, Your Highness." I answered vaguely, dropping my gaze. I wondered how much I should tell her about my family and the Gift, and I wished *Sabba* were here to advise me. But before I could say more, the princess abruptly began to tell me what she had dreamed last night.

In her dream, the princess had gone out into the garden with a piece of honey cake, intending to throw crumbs to a pet duckling. But at the pool she hardly recognized the duckling; he had grown from a fuzzy yellow baby into a strong-winged drake. Instead of swimming over to her to be fed, the drake paddled among the other ducks, stirring them up with his urgent quacking. Finally he flapped up into the air, circled the pool once, and flew off to the east. The whole flock followed him, leaving the princess all alone.

"And then I woke up," finished Princess Bint-Anath. "So sad! It was as sad as your song about Adam and Eve. I stayed in the garden, but I lost the one I loved most." She stared straight ahead, her eyes filling with tears as she remembered. "Nebet said I had been sobbing in my sleep, as if my heart would break."

To stop my hands from trembling, I massaged the oil harder into the princess's shoulders. I was as shaken by the dream as Princess Bint-Anath was, only for a different reason. The power of her dream reminded me that I had not dreamed like that since I left my village, more than a year ago. And yet I was the one with the Gift, was I not?

"Tell me more about Djo-sef's gift of interpreting dreams," the princess was saying. "Are there any Hebrews who have that gift in these times?"

My heart pounded. "Now and then, they say, one of Joseph's descendants will have the Gift."

I felt the muscles in her left shoulder tense under my hands. "If there is such a person, he must be found, to advise — " She broke off, for her chief lady-in-waiting was moving rapidly toward us. "Nebet, dear. No one could be more attentive than you."

I was glad to slip away from the stern at Lady Nebet's nod of dismissal. My head was whirling. I wondered if Princess Bint-Anath's dream *was* a message, but not for the princess. Maybe it was a message for me — for my clan. Suppose that the duckling stood for Moshe, whom she often called her duckling. Then the dream could be a reassurance that Moshe would grow up to lead his people.

But why would God speak to the Hebrews through an Egyptian princess? Why would He send such a dream to Princess Bint-Anath instead of to me, or *Sabba*, or anyone else of our clan?

Then another thought struck me, so bold that it made me shiver. How dare I think it? Such boldness would surely be punished! . . . And yet, did it not make sense?

This was my thought: If we had to wait for Moshe to grow up and become a second Joseph, the Hebrews would suffer for many more years. But I, Miri, would soon be a woman. I was learning the ways of Egyptian power. I could be the second Joseph.

CHAPTER 26

Like a Daughter

Floodtime passed, then the growing season, and it was harvest time, *shemu*, again. One afternoon in Princess Bint-Anath's garden, Nebet permitted herself a few minutes of relaxation. After all, everything was going so well. Look how happy the princess was, playing with Mose. Squealing, he toddled around and around a palm tree while the princess followed, pretending to snap at him like a crocodile.

Mose was a healthy, handsome little boy. He did not speak many words as yet, but he had a charming way about him. All the ladies loved him — although of course they would have pretended to dote on him in any case.

In another six months, Mose would be old enough to wean. Nebet had already set in motion extensive preparations for his adoption ceremony, to be held on the date declared propitious by the King's astrologer. Soon Nebet would present the princess with her suggestions for Mose's official name. It should include something flattering to the King, such as "Rameses-is-gracious," and something indicating where Mose had come from — "gift-of-Osiris" would be fitting.

A dry, restless wind rattled the palm fronds in the garden. Nebet glanced at the sky above the southern wall. Yes, there was a brownish haze, the sign of a *khamsin* approaching. But usually such *khamsins* veered off into the Great Eastern Desert without troubling Pharaoh's palace at Pi-Rameses.

Nebet's gaze turned to Mery, sitting in the shade of the jasmine arbor with the hairdresser. On a whim, Princess Bint-Anath had ordered Senen to arrange Mery's hair in the rows of tiny braids that were the fashion just now. So the hairdresser had spent much of the afternoon plaiting the girl's thick, dark hair. She had also replaced Mery's small earrings with her showy copper ones, shaped like crescents. Now, while Mery knelt in front of Senen with her eyes closed, the hairdresser stroked green paint on her lower eyelids.

The princess, letting Mose escape for the moment, paused in front of the jasmine arbor to consider the hairdresser's work. "Very nice! Did I not say that style would suit the girl? Mery, you shall attend me, looking just so, at the dedication of the new royal library."

Nebet smiled. Mery had won another favor from the princess. The untutored village girl Nebet had first met two years ago had all but vanished. In her place stood an accomplished young woman who had mastered the manners and unspoken rules of the court. At the same time, she still had that quality that could not be taught, an air of quiet confidence. This quality, together with her grace and her doe-eyed charm, would assure Mery of a good position as a lady's servant, even if the princess tired of her. And later, a suitable marriage could be arranged; Nebet had a certain scribe in mind.

Mery wore white linen all the time now, except in the servants' quarters. Nebet had been told that the girl stopped in the music-practice courtyard to change back into her striped Hebrew tunic before rejoining her mother, but that did not concern Nebet. Soon enough the Hebrew woman, her work as wet nurse finished, would be sent back to her village. Then Mery would feel no need to wear the Hebrew garment at all.

Nebet had gotten into the habit of talking things over with Mery. That is, Nebet talked and Mery listened. After years of keeping her own counsel, Nebet was surprised at the pleasure she took in explaining to the girl how she assessed various situations. For instance, Nebet had been wondering if the current tension between the oldest son of the King's second wife and the Grand Vizier's favorite concubine could be exploited, motivating both of them to give Mose rich gifts at his adoption celebration.

Mery did not have Nebet's deep knowledge of palace politics, of course. But she caught on quickly, and she seemed to understand the basic principles by

173

which Nebet worked. "A small wrestler, using his light weight with skill, can throw the strongest man," Nebet instructed her.

As the sun-barge of Amon-Re sank toward the western wall, Princess Bint-Anath prepared to leave the garden to dress for dinner. Mery took Mose from the princess and stood aside while the princess led her ladies back to her chambers. Then Mery, leading Mose by the hand, began to leave, but Nebet called her back.

"Stay here by the pool a moment; I wish to speak to you." It warmed Nebet's heart to see the girl's face light up. Mery enjoyed her lessons in palace politics as much as Nebet did.

Nebet crossed the garden to the shrine behind the tamarisks and bowed to the statue of Taweret. Usually she thought no more about making her regular offering to the hippopotamus goddess than she would about paying her informers. But today, raising her eyes to the heavy face, Nebet was struck with a new idea.

Perhaps Taweret had granted not only Nebet's prayer for the princess, but an unspoken prayer *for Nebet herself.* A desire so deep in Nebet's heart that she had not recognized it until this moment: the desire for a daughter.

Once admitted, the desire seized Nebet almost painfully, as if she were so thirsty that it was difficult to swallow the water she craved. She stared at the image of Taweret, stunned. Could it be that she, clever Lady Nebet, had been ungrateful to, even scornful of, the very deity who understood her inmost wish?

Overcome with emotion, Nebet stayed at the shrine for a few moments to compose herself. When she returned to the pool, she was surprised to find someone else in the garden besides Mery and Mose: the wigmaker, one of her most reliable informers.

The wigmaker bowed low. "Greetings, my lady." He was breathing heavily, as if he had run all the way to the garden. "I have news." He glanced sideways at Mery.

"I will speak with you later," Nebet told Mery. Judging from his expression, the wigmaker thought his news was important. When the girl had disappeared through the garden gate, Nebet nodded for him to begin.

THE WIGMAKER'S news was indeed important. And it was very bad. The High Priest of Amon-Re had arrived in Pi-Rameses for an unexpected visit.

With his formal leopard skin over his shoulders, the High Priest had gone straight to the King's audience hall. He announced that Amon-Re had led him here with a prophetic dream about a terrible danger to Pharaoh. The dream foretold that the Hebrews would rise up against the ruler of Upper and Lower Egypt, led by a Hebrew living in Pharaoh's own household!

The King had replied respectfully, but he had been obviously reluctant to agree that he might actually be in any danger. No doubt he could see where the High Priest was headed with this warning.

"Guided by Amon-Re the All-Seeing," the High

Priest had announced to the assembled court, "I personally, Your Majesty (may you live and prosper), aided by my most trusted priests, will scour your entire palace for Hebrews."

The wigmaker did a fair imitation of the High Priest's hollow tones, like a voice from a tomb, but Nebet could not take time to appreciate it. "When?" she snapped.

"Even as we speak, lady," answered the wigmaker. "I passed the stableyard on my way here, and one of his priests was already interrogating the grooms and chariot drivers."

This meant disaster unless Nebet acted quickly, quickly. Still, she did not neglect to slip an onyx ring from her finger and toss it to the wigmaker. If she rewarded her informers only for good news, then they would bring only good news, and she would not be well informed.

Nebet's mind whirled forward like the swiftest chariot wheel as she hastened out the garden gate and through the colonnades. The Hebrew nurse must be sent away immediately. Mose would have to be placed with another nurse — yes, the concubine Sitamun's child had just been weaned. That nurse — Kawit — would do, if she had not left the palace already.

Mery — must she go, too? Nebet felt a wrench at her heart.

THE LADY-IN-WAITING caught up with Mery in the music courtyard. Mose toddled over the tiles, chasing a cricket, as Mery knelt to place her lute in its basket. Holding her striped Hebrew tunic and one of the copper earrings, she looked up in surprise at Nebet in the doorway.

Nebet felt another wrench at her heart. No. She would *not* send this girl away forever. It would be difficult and costly to keep her, but Nebet would arrange it.

"Leave that," said Nebet to Mery, pointing to the tunic. "Listen carefully. There is not a moment to lose. The High Priest of Amon-Re is searching the palace for Hebrews. Mose's nurse must be sent to the docks immediately, to take a boat back to her village." Nebet gestured for Mery to rise. "Come, bring Mose. I will instruct you on the way to the servants' quarters."

Mery caught up the little boy and followed Nebet out of the courtyard. "My lady," she said in a choked tone, "perhaps there is a way for Mose to stay in the palace? His nurse and I could hide him for a time — yes, we could take him out to the pastures at the edge of the Eastern Desert, where our people keep flocks. We could wait until the High Priest leaves Pi-Rameses, and then — "

"Be still," said Nebet, though not unkindly. She was pleased that Mery's first reaction was to make a plan, however unrealistic. "I have already thought it through. There is no reason for Mose to leave the palace. Everyone knows that he is the miracle child, sent to her highness by Osiris. He will be well cared for by an Egyptian nurse."

Looking bewildered, Mery hugged Mose tightly. Nebet put a sympathetic hand on her shoulder. "So

you, too, must go to the docks, but not with the Hebrew woman. Wait until after sunset in the music
courtyard. I will send a guard to lead you to the
Mycenaean merchant's ship. The merchant owes me
a favor, and I will make all the arrangements.

"Once across the Great Sea, you will stay with the
merchant's family. After some time, you will return
with his ship — disguised as a maiden from Doria, to
the far north. Then I will hire you as my handmaiden.
As long as you never speak Hebrew, no one will be the
wiser."

Nebet swept through the gate of the servants'
quarters, beckoning to the housekeeper. "Is Kawit still
in the palace? Go, find her." Then she turned to Mery.
"Go tell Mose's wet nurse what she must do."

The Hebrew nurse was waiting in the courtyard,
and Nebet feared she would raise a fuss about leaving
Mose. As Nebet instructed a guard, she kept an eye on
Mery and her mother.

Yes, her *mother*. Nebet did not often catch sight of
the Hebrew woman, and usually she did not think of
her as Mery's mother. But now, seeing both of them
together, she could not escape the thought. As Mery
spoke to the woman in their own tongue, the afternoon light slanting across the courtyard touched their
faces, bringing out a resemblance.

The Hebrew woman stood with a stony expression while Mery, holding the boy, explained the emer-
gency and what Nebet had decided. When the girl
paused, the Hebrew nurse took Mose's head in her
hands and kissed him. Then, stepping back, she fixed

Mery with her large, dark eyes and spoke in a low, intense voice. Nebet did not understand the words, but it was clear, both from the way the woman bit them off and the way Mery flinched, that they were harsh.

The Egyptian nurse, Kawit, appeared and took Mose from Mery's arms. Mose was not a fussy child, but he must have sensed something was wrong. Whimpering, he held his arms out toward the Hebrew woman.

Nebet had instructed the guard to escort the Hebrew nurse away by force if necessary. But she only cast one last yearning glance at Mose before drawing her shawl over her head and turning toward the gate.

"*Imma!*" implored Mery.

The Hebrew woman stepped through the gateway. Then she stopped and turned, speaking through sobs. The guard took her arm, but she raised her other hand and spoke a few words as if in blessing. "*Shalom*, Miriam." Then she was gone.

The girl stood very still, looking after her. It struck Nebet how young Mery really was, in spite of her maturity and intelligence. "Come, be brave, little one." Nebet stepped forward and touched her shoulder tenderly, as if Mery were indeed her own daughter about to leave home. In a whisper she added, "The months will go quickly, and then, Hathor willing, you will return to Pi-Rameses to stay."

CHAPTER 27

I Am Miriam

מרים

I stood in the middle of the servants' courtyard, as stunned as if *Imma* had slapped my face. *This is not my daughter, this girl in the shameless dress, this girl with painted eyelids*, she had said, looking me up and down. *This is an Egyptian dancing girl named Mery*. And she had turned to leave with the guard. When she was almost out of the gate, I cried out, *"Imma!"*

Then my mother turned back, and I saw her tears. "God pity me!" she cried. "To lose a son and a daughter on the same black day!" Before the guard could pull her away, she raised a hand and added, *"Shalom*, Miriam. Go with God."

At least *Imma* had given me her blessing. But she did not understand. She blamed me — she did not realize that I had no choice. I had to do what Lady

Nebet said in order to stay in the palace with Moshe. I began to sob out loud, standing in the middle of the courtyard with the other servants watching curiously.

Then there were voices at the gate, and a priest and his guards pushed into the servants' quarters. Fear dried my eyes.

Beckoning to the housekeeper, the priest began to question her. Even in my misery I was amused to think that he would get no secrets out of *her*. The housekeeper was one of Lady Nebet's informers.

The priest gestured at me, and my heart skipped a beat. "Oh, her," said the housekeeper. "That silly Mery is blubbering over a lost earring, and only a copper one at that."

I managed to pick up the cue, putting my hand to my ear. "My earring!" I sobbed. But I was thinking of my mother disappearing through the gate.

Losing interest in me, the priest stalked on around the courtyard. He had the housekeeper name each woman and child. I watched out of the corner of my eye, holding my breath as the priest ran his eyes over Mose and Kawit. She was feeding him bits of honey cake, and he was quiet for the moment.

Lady Nebet had acted just in time, I realized with a shudder. A few moments more, and my mother in her striped wool tunic and head scarf would have been an easy catch for the Theban priest. I prayed that she was safely on a boat by now, on her way up the river.

Finally the priest and his guards left, without another glance at me. As far as they were concerned, I was just another Egyptian girl.

An Egyptian dancing girl named Mery. Remembering my mother's parting words, even her sarcastic attempt at an Egyptian accent when she said "Mery," I caught my breath in pain. I had been so proud, ever since the trip to Thebes, that I could fool anyone into thinking I was Egyptian. My accent was perfect, my clothes a cunning costume. But if my own mother thought I had turned into an Egyptian girl —

Perhaps it was myself I had fooled.

Slaves were beginning to bring out the evening meal, and the servants settled down on the benches to eat. Kawit said kindly to me, "Come, Mery, take food. You will feel better once your stomach is full."

I managed to smile weakly at her, but I only wanted to be by myself. Murmuring something about an errand for Lady Nebet, I left the courtyard.

My excuse was truthful enough, because I found myself heading for the music-practice courtyard. Lady Nebet had told me to wait there for my escort. It was also a good place to be alone, because it was deserted at this hour.

Sitting down on a bench, I watched the sky darken. I remembered again the way my mother had looked at me, her usually gentle eyes turned hard and narrow. Had she not seen her daughter Miri under the white linen shift and eye paint?

Maybe my mother had seen more than the outside. Maybe she had looked inside and seen changes as clear as a white shift and green eye paint. Once I sang only hymns to the Lord God or songs of my people's heroes. Now I sang of the gods Osiris and

182

Hathor or of an idle lady longing for her lover. I impatiently turned away from *Imma*'s advice but eagerly looked forward to instruction from Lady Nebet.

On the day I left for the palace, I had promised Tamar I would come back for her wedding. But in fact, I had not even remembered the wedding. I was as bad as my faithless sister, Leah.

With the shock of that thought, I began to sob out loud again. I had indeed become foreign, not just to others but to myself.

Searching for a reassuring sight, I looked up at the night sky, blazing with stars. But I quickly dropped my gaze. Could the stars now be, for me, the descendants God had promised Abraham? Perhaps it would not be long before I saw only the spangles on the robe of the sky-goddess Nut. What if I was trapped forever in the Egyptians' world, turned into the "Mery" painted on the wall of Princess Bint-Anath's tomb?

"I am not an Egyptian girl!" I said it out loud, to hear it with my own ears. "I am Miriam, daughter of Amram and Jochabed, granddaughter of Kohath, sister of Aaron and Moshe, niece of Hebron and Shiphrah, cousin of Tamar and Ephraim and Rachel. Miriam, of the clan of Levi."

But how could I remain Miriam all by myself? After I had crossed the Great Sea on a ship and lived with the Mycenaeans for a time and then returned to Pi-Rameses to become Lady Nebet's handmaiden — what would be left of Miri? Lady Nebet had said I must give up speaking Hebrew. How, then, could I become a second Joseph? I would not even be able to teach Moshe — *Mose*, now, forever — the prayers as he grew up.

With a deep, shuddering sigh, I again lifted my face to the sky over the courtyard. "Lord God, it is me, your Miriam. I am all alone. Do not leave me!"

A quiet voice spoke in my head, cutting through the frantic thoughts. *You are the one who is planning to leave, Miriam.*

I had not seen it that way. It was Lady Nebet's idea for me to flee across the Great Sea and return next year as a foreigner. Was I wrong to think I owed her obedience? She was Princess Bint-Anath's chief lady-in-waiting, after all, and I was a mere servant girl. Besides, she was wise, and I knew she had my best interests at heart. She intended to teach me and bring me along in the princess's court. And if I obeyed her, I could come back to Moshe.

But what if I chose not to follow Lady Nebet's plan? What about God's plan for me? I had thought I understood it. But surely that was foolish, presuming to guess the ways of the One who set the stars in the sky and the peoples on the earth.

After the trip to Thebes, I had waited for the princess to consult me again about her dreams. But she had never mentioned dreams or "Djo-sef" to me again. Once I casually asked Lady Nebet if her highness ever had nightmares these days. "Indeed, no," she had replied in a reproving tone, "although if she had, it should not be a subject of gossip among her servants." Was I really supposed to become a second Joseph, then — or was I to use my Gift in a different way?

Did I still have the Gift?

I tried not to dwell on that last question. I remembered how *Sabba* had told me to ask for guidance. "Have an open and waiting spirit." I closed my eyes and quieted my breathing. And I felt the regular beat of my heart. I waited.

CHAPTER 28

Miriam's Home

מרים

In the scene that unfolded in my mind, it was still evening. But I was not in the palace, but rather out in the pastureland at the edge of the Eastern Desert. Tents, and the campfires between them, crowded the shallow bowl of the valley where the Hebrew clans gathered for the shearing festival. The night air was dry and chill, but I was warm in a wool tunic and headscarf.

At the bottom of the valley, a man raised his arms and spoke to the gathering. His voice rang from the slopes, and the great assembly was hushed, listening. I glowed with pride, for the man was my brother Aaron.

Then Aaron finished, and I stepped forward. I struck my timbrel. "We are only visitors in Egypt," I sang. "The Lord will lead us to our homeland." I began to dance, and the women followed me, weaving among the tents until all the assembled clans were one fabric.

WHEN I OPENED my eyes, I felt calm. I did not know how the vision would come about, but I was deeply grateful for the glimpse of a future in which I was myself, and with Aaron, and using the Gift for our people. At least I could plan what to do right now, to go forward toward that future. I took my Hebrew tunic from the lute basket and touched the strings of the lute in farewell. Lifting a timbrel from a peg in the storage room, I wrapped it in my tunic.

A short time later, a man with a torch appeared in the door of the courtyard. I recognized him as one of the princess's guards — this must be the man Lady Nebet had sent to take me to the docks. He nodded at me without speaking; I nodded back and picked up my bundle.

As I followed him along the arcade, he put out his torch. We kept to the shadows, passing the guest quarters where the High Priest of Amon-Re was staying. For hours, it seemed, we stole along behind the stockyards and the cookhouses, until finally we left the palace grounds through a small side gate. Now I could see well enough to pick my way over a refuse pile and around to the steps below the front gates of the palace.

Down at the river, ships rocked at their moorings. The guard pointed to a ship of seagoing size with a foreign design. "The Mycenaean."

I nodded and started for the ship he had pointed out. But as soon as the guard had disappeared through the palace gates, I turned and walked along the docks to a cargo barge. I had never been all by myself at night in the city, and now I was walking away from the protection of Lady Nebet's arrangements. I trembled, and I prayed for courage. If the barge was headed up the river, and if they had room for a passenger, and if the captain did not think a girl traveling alone should be reported to the palace guard . . .

But the captain of the barge did not seem concerned about who I was or where I had come from. Yes, he was going upriver in the morning, he said. And he did not mind taking one of my copper bangles in trade for a ride as far as Sir Satepihu's estate.

The rest of the night I spent on a pile of empty grain sacks in a corner of the deck. I had changed into my striped tunic, and pillowed my head on the rolled-up linen shift. Its scent of lotus perfume was like a message: *Think what you are leaving behind.*

I was leaving luxury: slaves to grind wheat for my bread and wash my laundry; food fine enough for a festival at home, as much as I wished; new clothes to wear, and jewelry to set them off; a palace full of wonders to explore; the daily pleasure of music practice; the daily beauty of the princess's garden. Yet what I would miss far more was Lady Nebet's approving glance. I wished I could kneel before her and explain why I was leaving, but she would not understand. Had she not shown me the ways of power in Pi-Rameses? Had she not taught me to pay attention to what people care about most and to use that knowledge to gain advantage?

She had showed me, in fact, that I might become a second Joseph. And now I was deceiving her, leaving without a word. It would seem to her that I was flinging her gifts back in her face.

As these thoughts tormented me, I shifted restlessly back and forth. Every time I moved my head, a whiff of lotus floated up from the linen as a further torment.

Finally I fell asleep and dreamed:

I stood with Aaron and Moshe on the eastern shore of a sea. This was not the Great Sea to the north, but a shallow, marshy sea near the Eastern Desert. The sun was just rising over the hills behind us.

Both Moshe and Aaron were now grown men, but Moshe was not the Prince Mose of my imagination. His hair and full beard were as rough as a shepherd's, and he wore a sheepskin cloak over his patterned tunic. One hand held a staff; the other he stretched out toward the sea.

Below us the sea bed was empty, the incoming tide pushed back by a steady wind from the desert. Clumps of dry reeds rattled in the wind. Instead of water, my people flowed into the sea bed and out again, past me and Aaron and Moshe, like sheep flowing around their herders. Far behind in the west was Egypt — Egypt, and the brickyards, and the scribes with their cruel lists and tallies, and the stewards and the landlords, and the High Priests of Amon-Re, and Pharaoh himself.

IN THE MORNING, the dream stayed with me. I was on the cargo barge, sailing up the river, but I also seemed to be on the shore of that empty eastern sea. The dream felt as powerful as the current of the Nile, although I did not understand how it could ever come to pass.

How could the Hebrews, our loosely linked group of clans, bind together as a nation with one purpose?

How could Moshe, growing up as Princess Bint-Anath's son, become a great leader of his people?

How could a nation of thousands of men, women, and children, with all their sheep and goats, cross the vast eastern wilderness in safety?

How could the Egyptians be persuaded to release us, to give up the laborers who supported their way of life? If Pharaoh wanted to hold us here — I remembered the troops of foot soldiers training on the palace grounds, armed with long spears and protected with armor. I remembered the charioteers, aiming their arrows at targets as they thundered around the stable yard.

Yet to that last question, the hint of an answer came to my mind. It was something Lady Nebet had said to me: "A small wrestler, using his light weight with skill, can throw the strongest man."

From under the sail of the barge I tried to look east, in the direction of the Great Desert. But the morning sun, glittering on the water, hurt my eyes. Still, I felt drawn toward the east, as if I were a growing plant leaning toward light.

Before I knew it, the barge reached the canal at the

edge of Satepihu's estate. The captain paused close to the bank, and I jumped out and splashed through the mud of the papyrus marsh. Climbing up to the canal path, I hurried along the top of the dike.

Now I could see the rooftops of Demy-en-Osiris. There would be few people in the village in the middle of the morning; they would all be out in the wheat fields, harvesting.

The village looked smaller and dirtier than I had remembered. The god Osiris could not be very flattered to have such a miserable heap of mud-brick huts named after him. Had I given up the palace for this? Never again would I walk on smooth tile floors under cool arcades. Never again would I spend my mornings lost in chords and melodies, or my afternoons breathing the fragrance of jasmine and lotus.

In a short time I would be grinding barley and hauling water from the canal again. I ran my thumbs over the soft palms of my hands, seeming to feel the blisters already.

But although I was returning to the same village where I had been born, I was not the same. I was no longer a child, any more than Tamar — a married woman! — was a child. I felt a pang of longing for the days when Tamar and I were girls together. Those days were gone forever.

Still, here I was myself — Miriam. That cluster of mud huts was where my people lived, where they spent their days laboring for the Egyptians. After what I had seen of life at the palace, I knew how wrong this was.

As I paused on the edge of the Hebrew section of the village, a boy appeared from the direction of the fields. His arms were full of straw, and he looked sad. For just an instant I did not recognize him. Then I saw it was Aaron.

"*Shalom*, brother!" I called out.

"*Shalom* — Miri!" Aaron's face lit up, and even his curly hair seemed to spring farther out from his head. He had pronounced my name clearly, without any lisp. "*Imma* said you were not coming home."

"But here I am!" I said. My heart swelled so that I thought my chest would burst. "I am home with you for good."